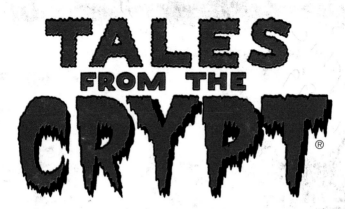

TALES FROM THE CRYPT®

NO. 8 – *Diary of a Stinky Dead Kid*

STEFAN PETRUCHA
MAIA KINNEY-PETRUCHA
JOHN L. LANSDALE
JIM SALICRUP
Writers

RICK PARKER
MIRAN KIM
JAMES ROMBERGER &
MARGUERITE VAN COOK
Artists

MR. EXES
Cover Artist

Based on the classic EC Comics series created by WILLIAM M. GAINES

PAPERCUTZ™
New York

"DIARY OF A STINKY DEAD KID"
PARTS ONE & TWO
STEFAN PETRUCHA – Writer
RICK PARKER – Artist, Letterer

"DIELITE"
**STEFAN PETRUCHA &
MAIA KINNEY-PETRUCHA** – Writers
MIRAN KIM – Artist
BRYAN SENKA – Letterer

"CARRIER"
JOHN L. LANSDALE – Writer
**JAMES ROMBERGER &
MARGUERITE VAN COOK** – Artists
MARK LERER – Letterer

GHOULUNATIC SEQUENCES
JIM SALICRUP – Writer
RICK PARKER – Artist, Title Letterer, Colorist
MARK LERER – Letterer

CHRIS NELSON & SHELLY DUTCHAK
Production

MICHAEL PETRANEK
Editorial Assistant

JIM SALICRUP
Editor-in-Chief

ISBN: 978-1-59707-163-5 paperback edition
ISBN: 978-1-59707-164-2 hardcover edition
Copyright © 2009 William M. Gaines, Agent, Inc. All rights reserved.
The EC logo is a registered trademark of William M. Gaines, Agent, Inc. used with permission.

Printed in Canada
November 2009 by Marquis Imprimeur Inc.
2700, rue Rachel est
Montreal, Quebec H2H 1S7

Distributed by Macmillan

10 9 8 7 6 5 4 3

THE CRYPT OF TERROR

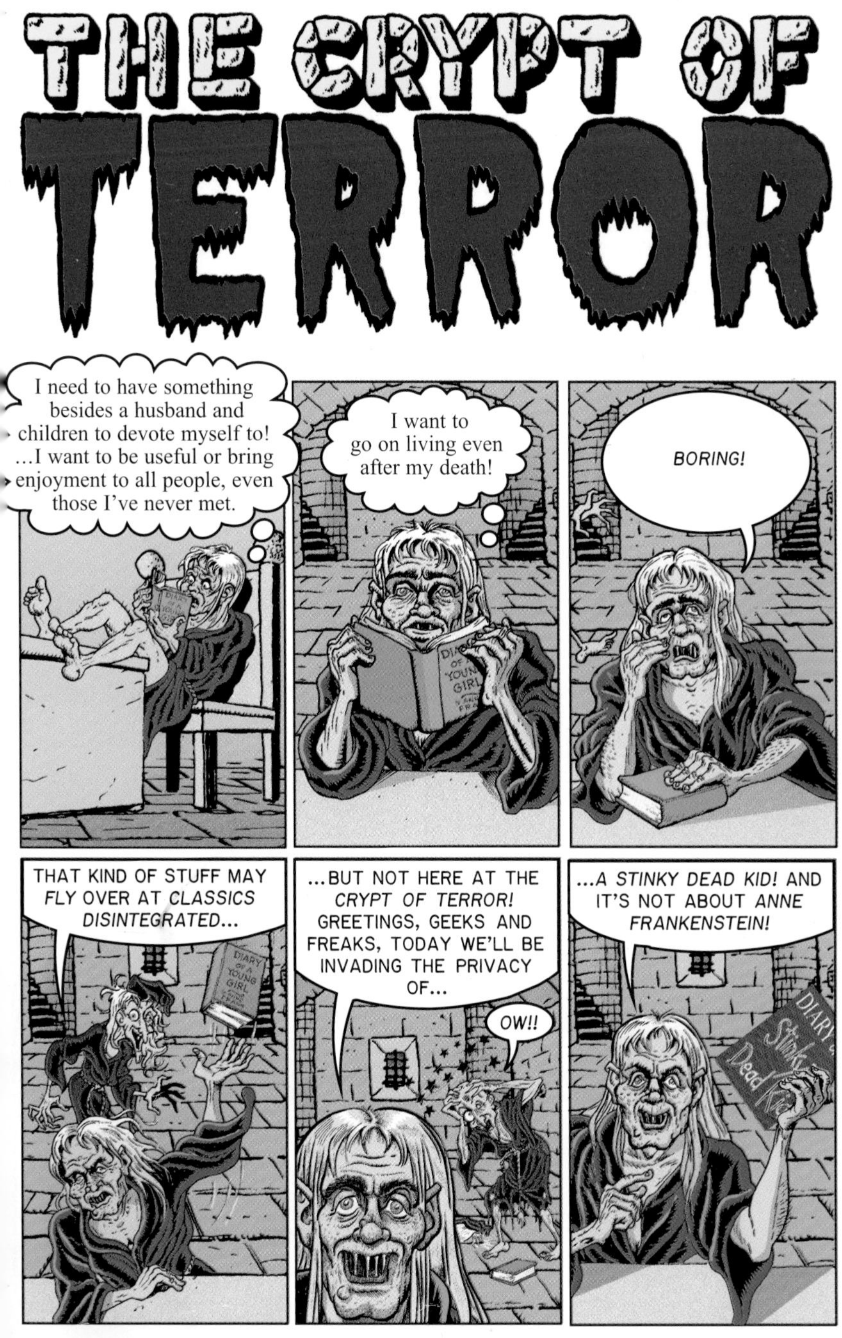

I need to have something besides a husband and children to devote myself to! ...I want to be useful or bring enjoyment to all people, even those I've never met.
I want to go on living even after my death!
BORING!
THAT KIND OF STUFF MAY *FLY* OVER AT *CLASSICS DISINTEGRATED*...
DIARY OF A YOUNG GIRL
...BUT NOT HERE AT THE *CRYPT OF TERROR!* GREETINGS, GEEKS AND FREAKS, TODAY WE'LL BE INVADING THE PRIVACY OF...
OW!!
...*A STINKY DEAD KID!* AND IT'S NOT ABOUT *ANNE FRANKENSTEIN!*

October

Monday

My name's Glugg. It's always sad and scary when a kid dies, especially if it's you. Funny, for the longest time I thought the scariest thing was my brother, Rock.

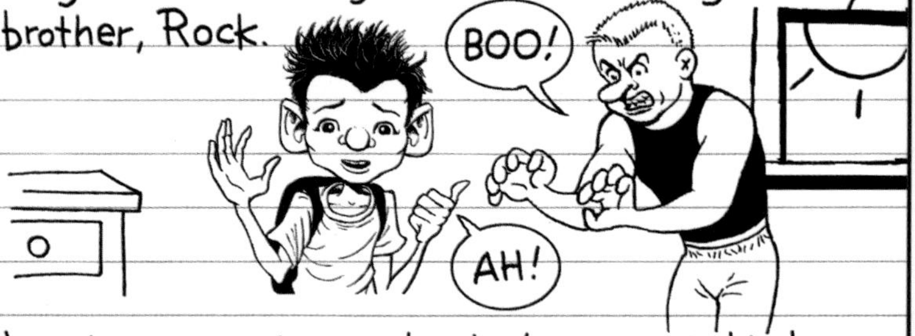
BOO!
AH!

He's twice my size and only has room in his brain for his band, bullying me and making fun of this journal. I think he's jealous I can write. Plus he wants a new drum set badly, and our parents made it clear we can't afford one.

Anyway, it turns out there ARE things scarier than Rock, just a couple, though, like death.

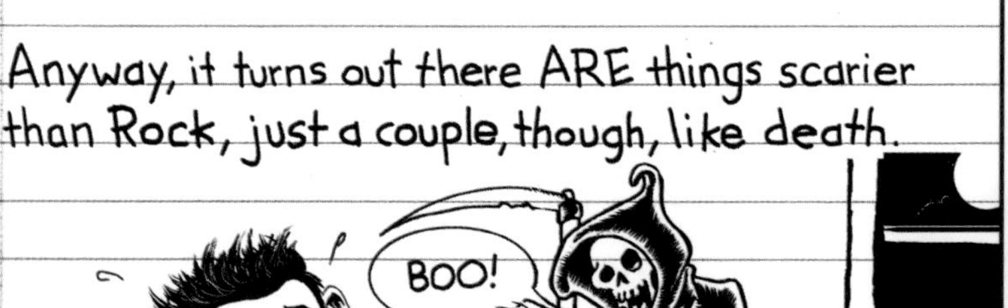
BOO!
AHHHH!

Have you ever just KNOWN the phone will ring and exactly who's calling and you feel really cool, like it's magic or something?

You'd think with something big as DEATH, you'd get the same kind of warning, but nope. Not me, anyway. No bells, no whistles, not even a vague sense of impending doom.

It sucks! I mean I was minding my own business, standing next to my pal Al Crowley at the train station with the rest of the kids, on our dumb school trip to the Museum, when...

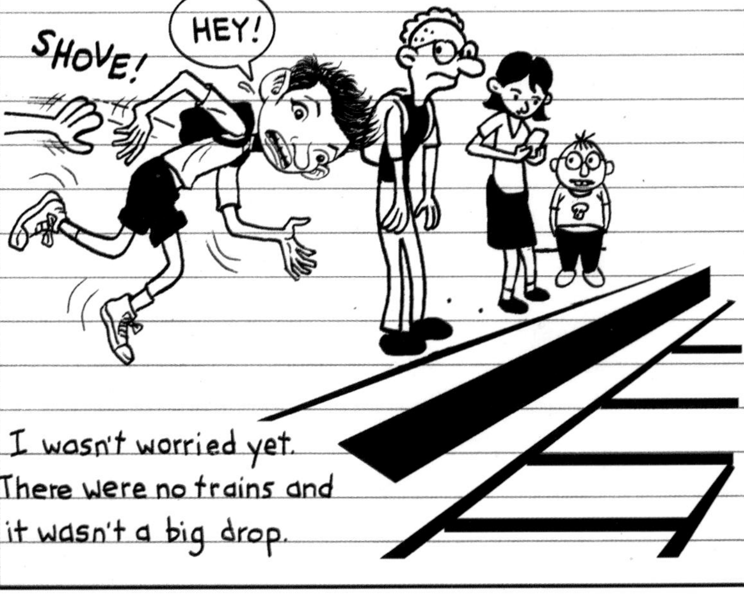
SHOVE!
HEY!

I wasn't worried yet. There were no trains and it wasn't a big drop.

After I hit bottom, I even managed to have a short chat with Crowley.

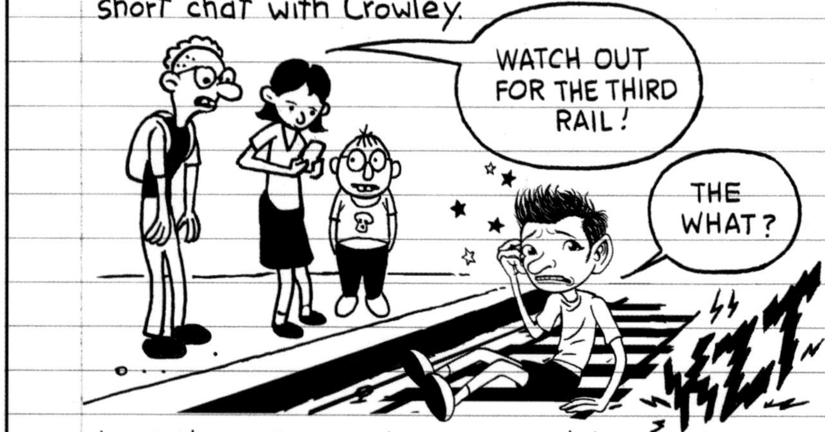
WATCH OUT FOR THE THIRD RAIL!
THE WHAT?
ZZZT!

Next thing I remember is a weird dream about being in my living room. Mom's dressed in robes and reading from an old book. She loves books.

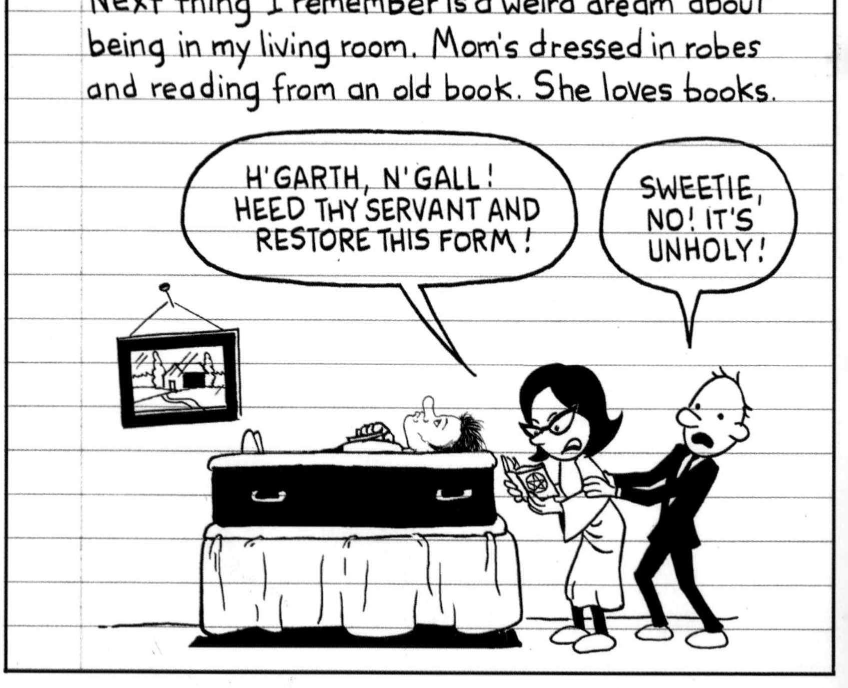
H'GARTH, N'GALL! HEED THY SERVANT AND RESTORE THIS FORM!
SWEETIE, NO! IT'S UNHOLY!

Me, I thought it was neat, but I guess Dad talked her out of it since it all went black again.

Tuesday

PART of the spell must've stuck, which made me REALLY wish Dad had let Mom finish.

I know people think it'd be cool to be at their own funeral, but I doubt they're imagining being totally paralyzed.

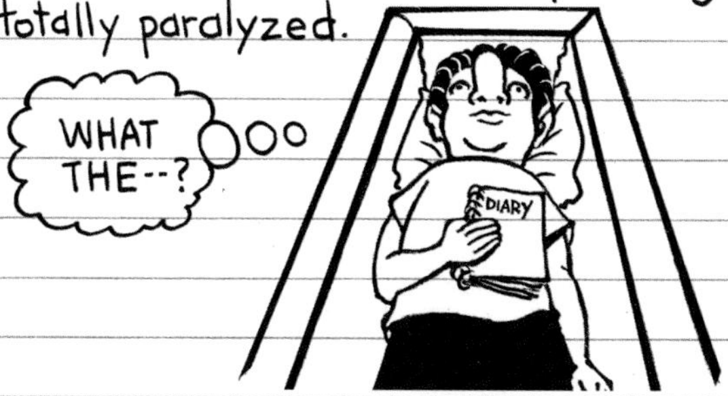

WHAT THE--?
DIARY

Worse? I could still SMELL! Uncle Garth, who always wears a gallon of awful cologne, leaned over my casket and said:

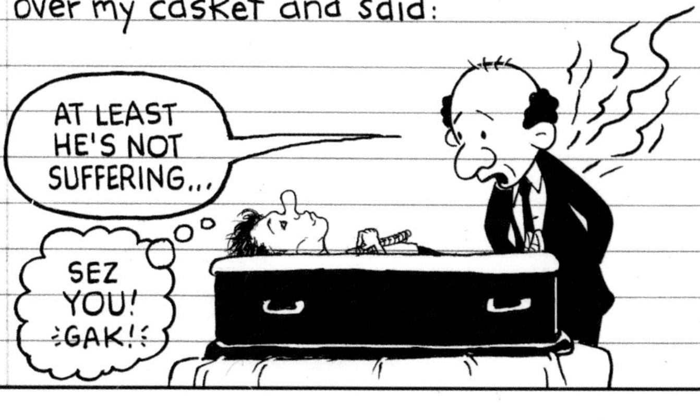

AT LEAST HE'S NOT SUFFERING...
SEZ YOU! :GAK!:

It did make me appreciate Crowley, sort of.

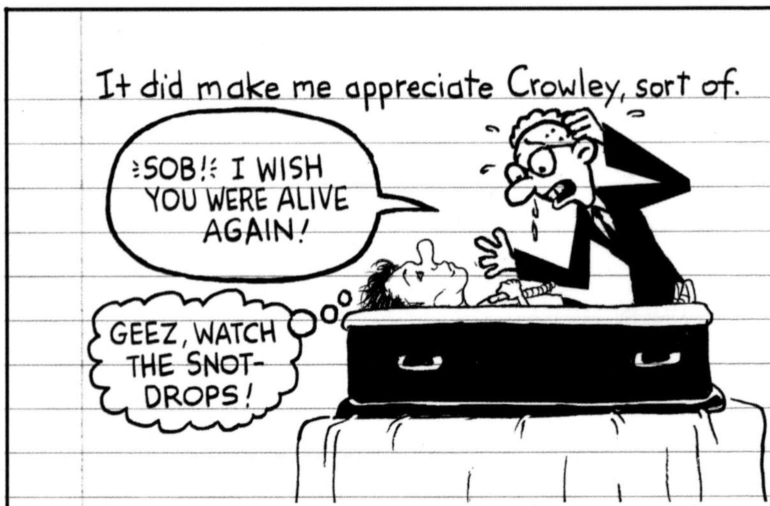
SOB! I WISH YOU WERE ALIVE AGAIN!
GEEZ, WATCH THE SNOT-DROPS!

The WEIRDEST part was Rock. He looked all sad, but I think that was just an act for Mom. Because then...

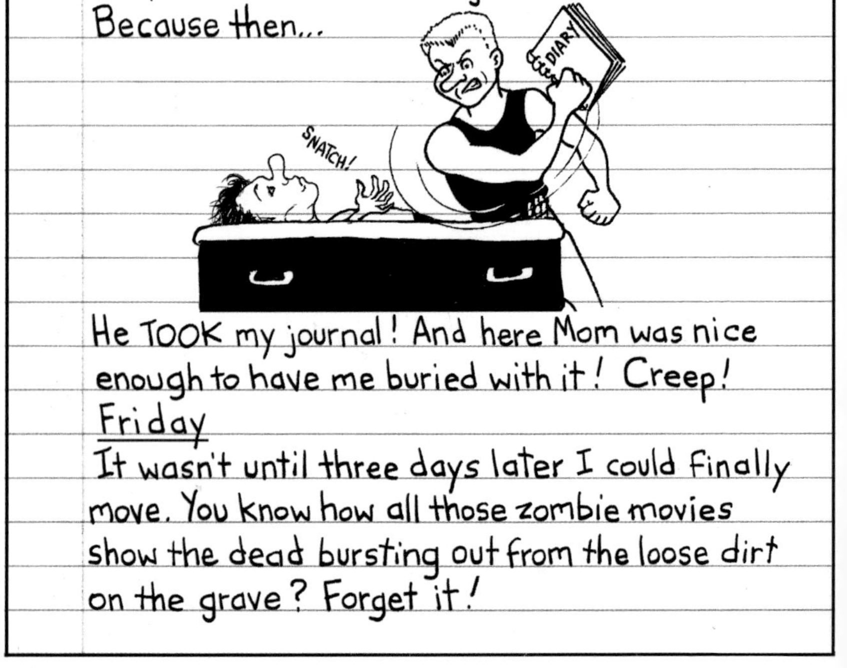
DIARY
SNATCH!

He TOOK my journal! And here Mom was nice enough to have me buried with it! Creep!

Friday

It wasn't until three days later I could finally move. You know how all those zombie movies show the dead bursting out from the loose dirt on the grave? Forget it!

Saturday

R.I.P.
GLUGG
2009

Sunday

R.I.P.
GLUGG
2009

Monday

R.I.P.
GLUGG
2009

Tuesday

R.I.P.
GLUGG
2009
PHEW!

Let me tell you, this stuff was packed! I didn't think I'd ever get the dirt out from under my nails!

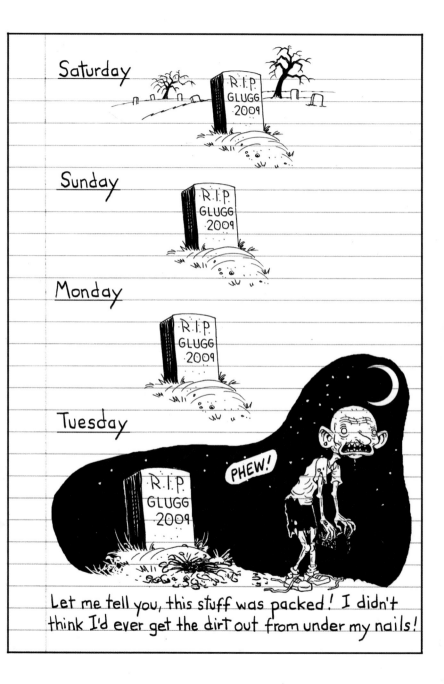

I was totally tired, but so glad to be out, I was feeling good. I even started wondering if there were any advantages to this zombie thing.

Would I live forever? Did I have to eat brains? Not that I was eager to find out. but they HAD to taste better than Mom's broccoli and Velveeta.

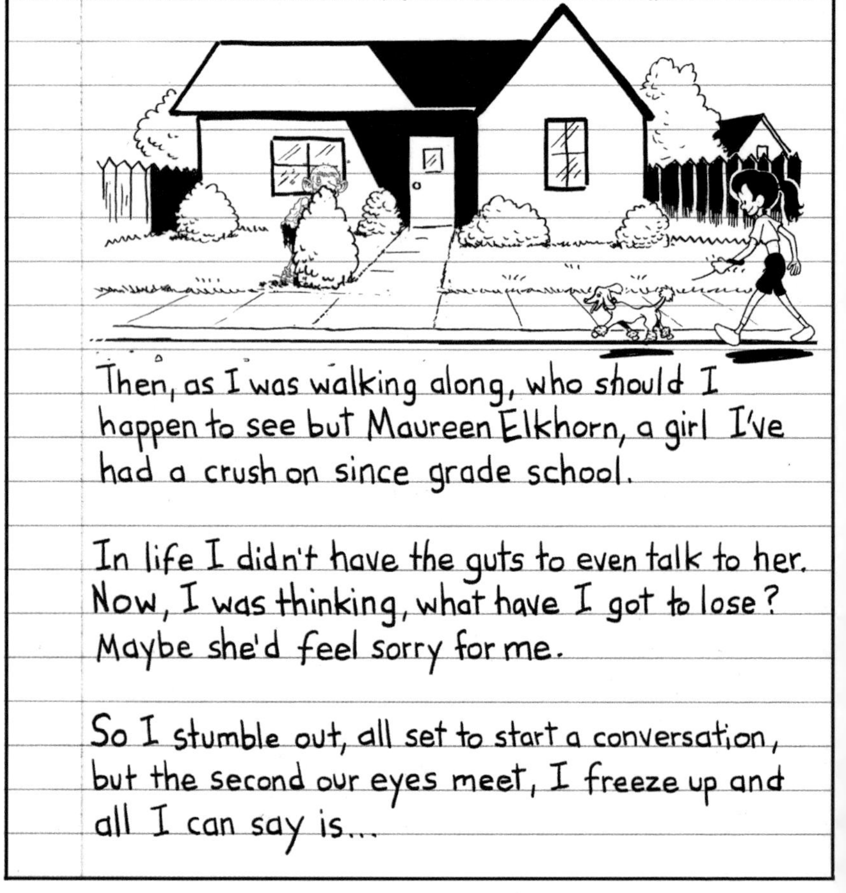

Then, as I was walking along, who should I happen to see but Maureen Elkhorn, a girl I've had a crush on since grade school.

In life I didn't have the guts to even talk to her. Now, I was thinking, what have I got to lose? Maybe she'd feel sorry for me.

So I stumble out, all set to start a conversation, but the second our eyes meet, I freeze up and all I can say is...

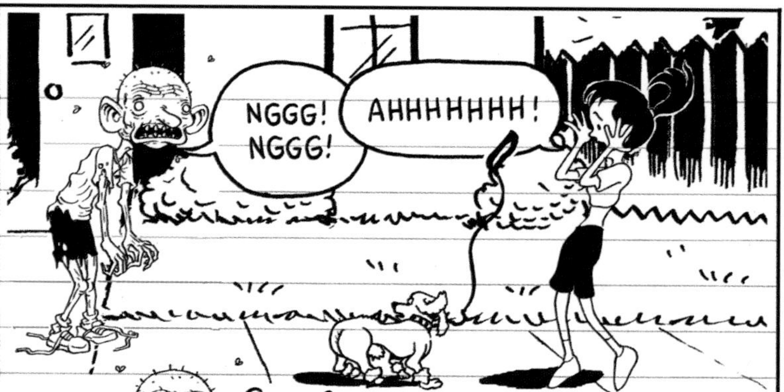
NGGG! NGGG!
AHHHHHHH!

So of course she ran away.

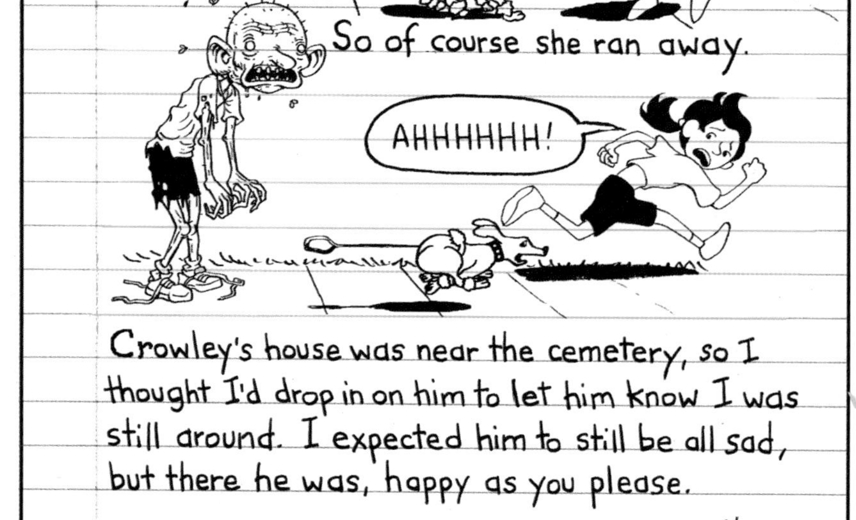
AHHHHHH!

Crowley's house was near the cemetery, so I thought I'd drop in on him to let him know I was still around. I expected him to still be all sad, but there he was, happy as you please.

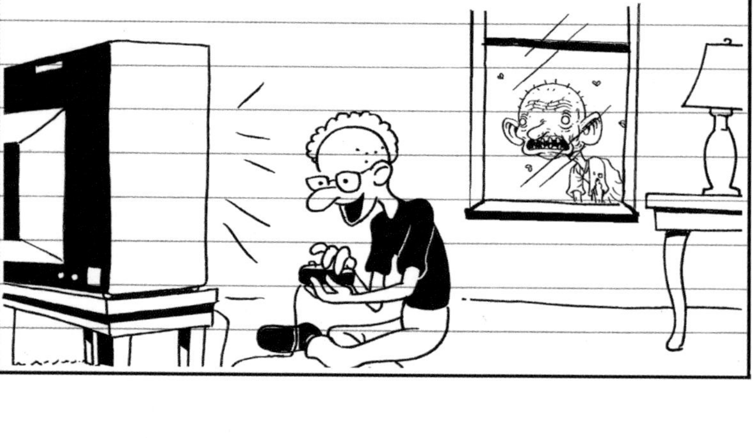

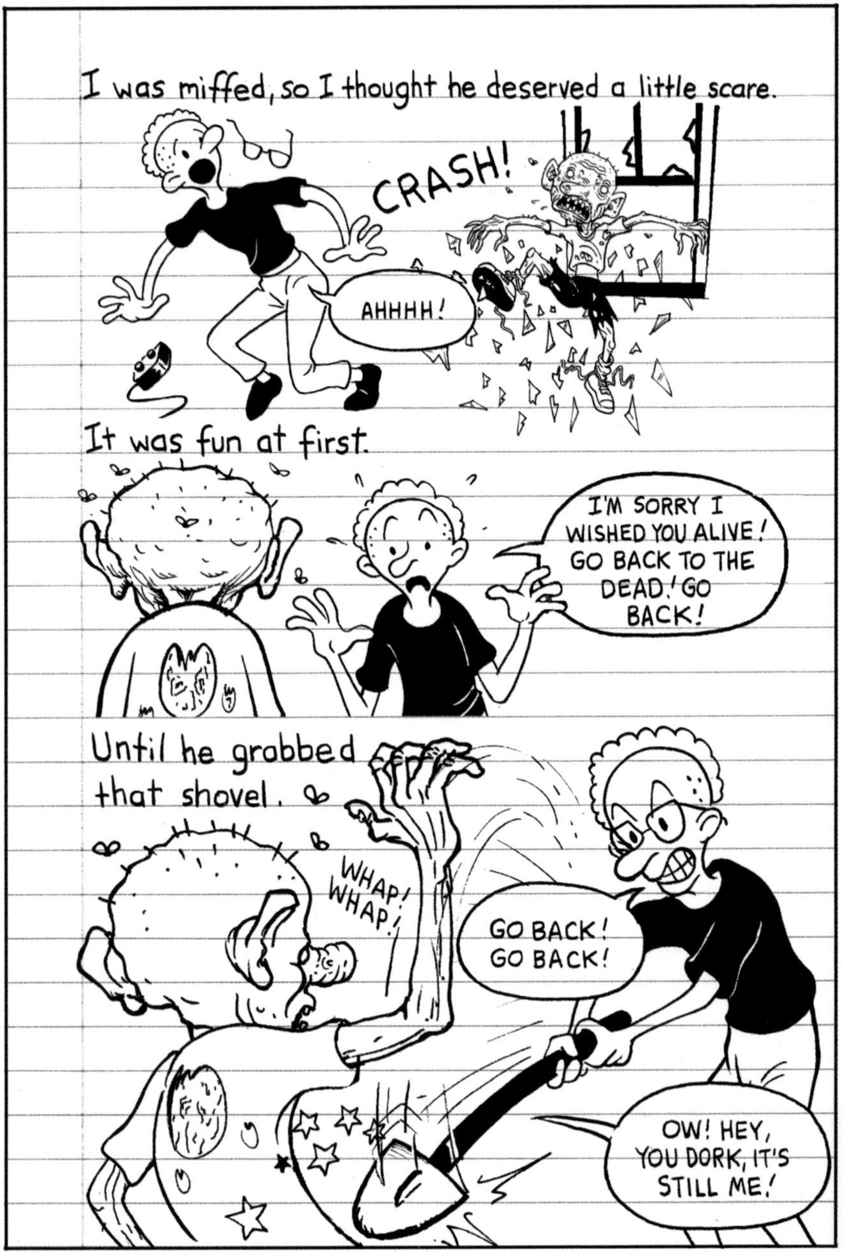
I was miffed, so I thought he deserved a little scare.
CRASH!
AHHHH!
It was fun at first.
I'M SORRY I WISHED YOU ALIVE! GO BACK TO THE DEAD! GO BACK!
Until he grabbed that shovel.
WHAP! WHAP!
GO BACK! GO BACK!
OW! HEY, YOU DORK, IT'S STILL ME!

Like Mom says, it's always fun until someone gets hurt, in this case, me!

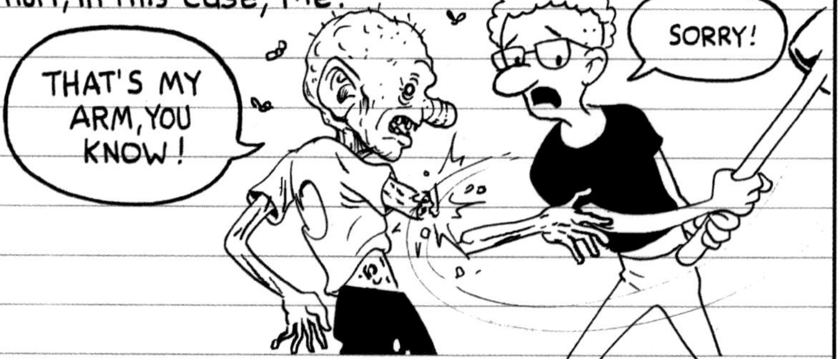
THAT'S MY ARM, YOU KNOW!
SORRY!

Once I promised not to eat his brain, he did feel bad about it. He ran all over the house, got needle and thread, crazy glue and duct tape, and tried to stick it back on.

It wasn't until he finished we noticed it was on backwards. Crowley's not the brightest bulb.

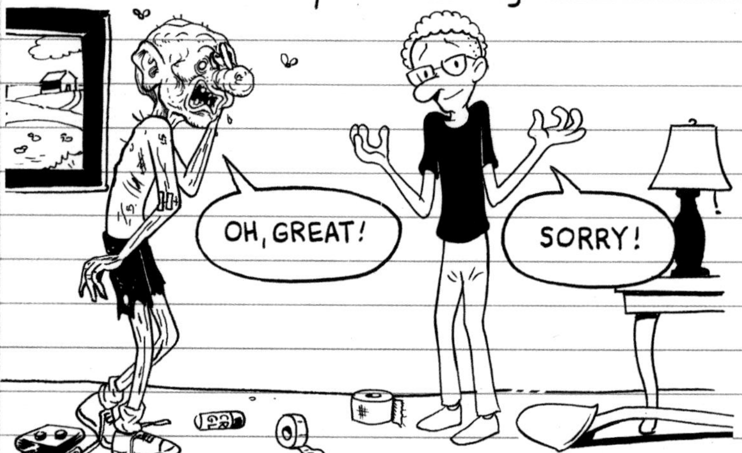
OH, GREAT!
SORRY!

He offered to break it off and start over, but by now I wanted to get home. He tried to shake my hand, but that only got me all angry again.

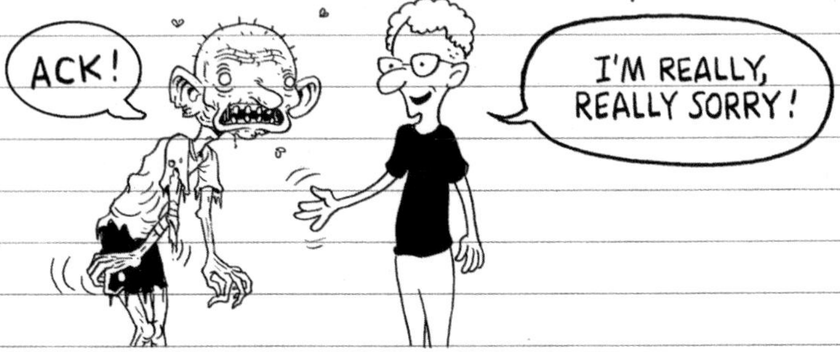
ACK!
I'M REALLY, REALLY SORRY!

My folks couldn't worry about me anymore, but I was thinking maybe Mom could use that book of hers to turn me into something cooler, like a vampire or a werewolf.

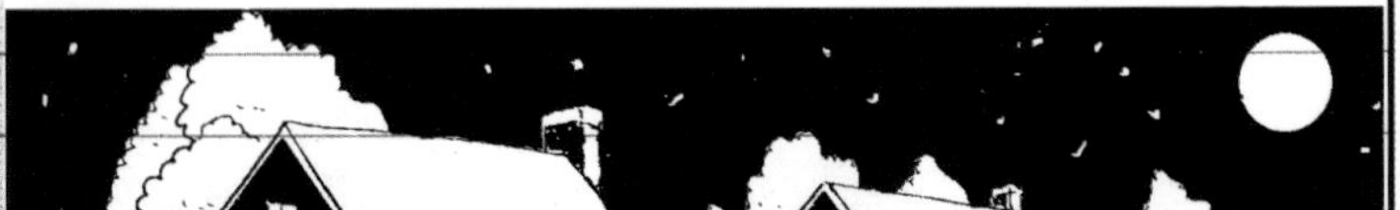

As I got near, I heard the puke-inducing sounds of my brother's band, *Rock and the Rock's Rock*, practicing in the basement, which meant Mom and Dad would be upstairs, wearing earplugs.

Given how Maureen and Crowley reacted to me, I thought it'd be cool to get back at Rock for all that bullying. It's not like I'd have to DO anything, which meant I couldn't wuss out. All I had to do was show my face.

But what do you know? He wasn't practicing! It was a tape playing! Rock had Mom's book AND my journal out, and he'd drawn a weird symbol on the floor.

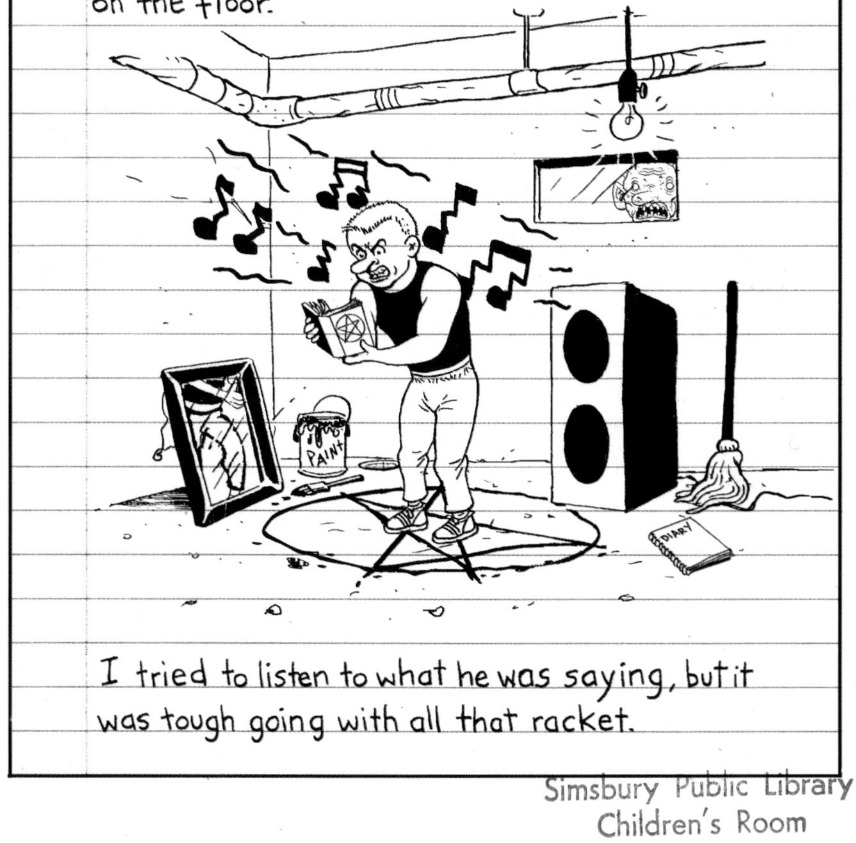
PAINT
DIARY

I tried to listen to what he was saying, but it was tough going with all that racket.

All of a sudden, there was a big burst of light, a smell like a week of bad farts and...

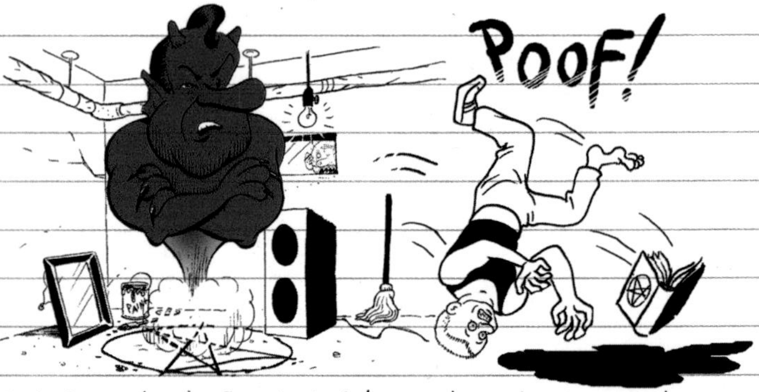
POOF!

I didn't think Rock had it in him, but somehow he'd managed to conjure a demon! I thought for a second maybe he was trying to help bring me back to life or something, but no...

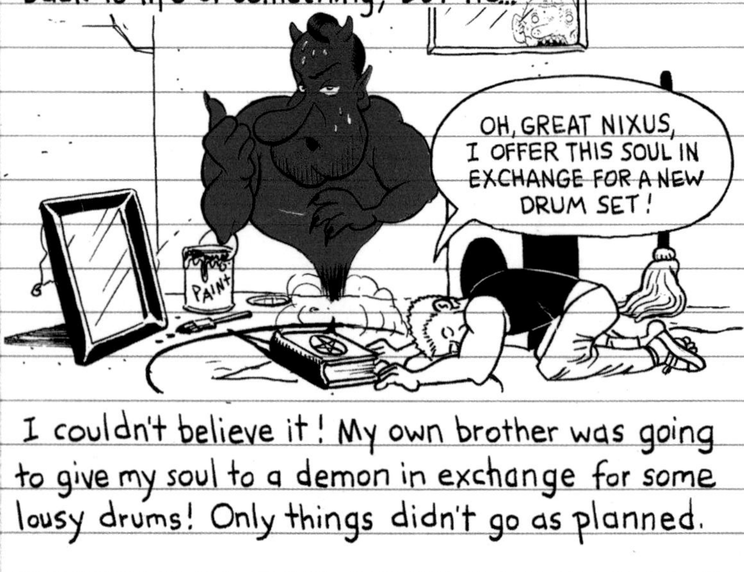
OH, GREAT NIXUS, I OFFER THIS SOUL IN EXCHANGE FOR A NEW DRUM SET!
PAINT

I couldn't believe it! My own brother was going to give my soul to a demon in exchange for some lousy drums! Only things didn't go as planned.

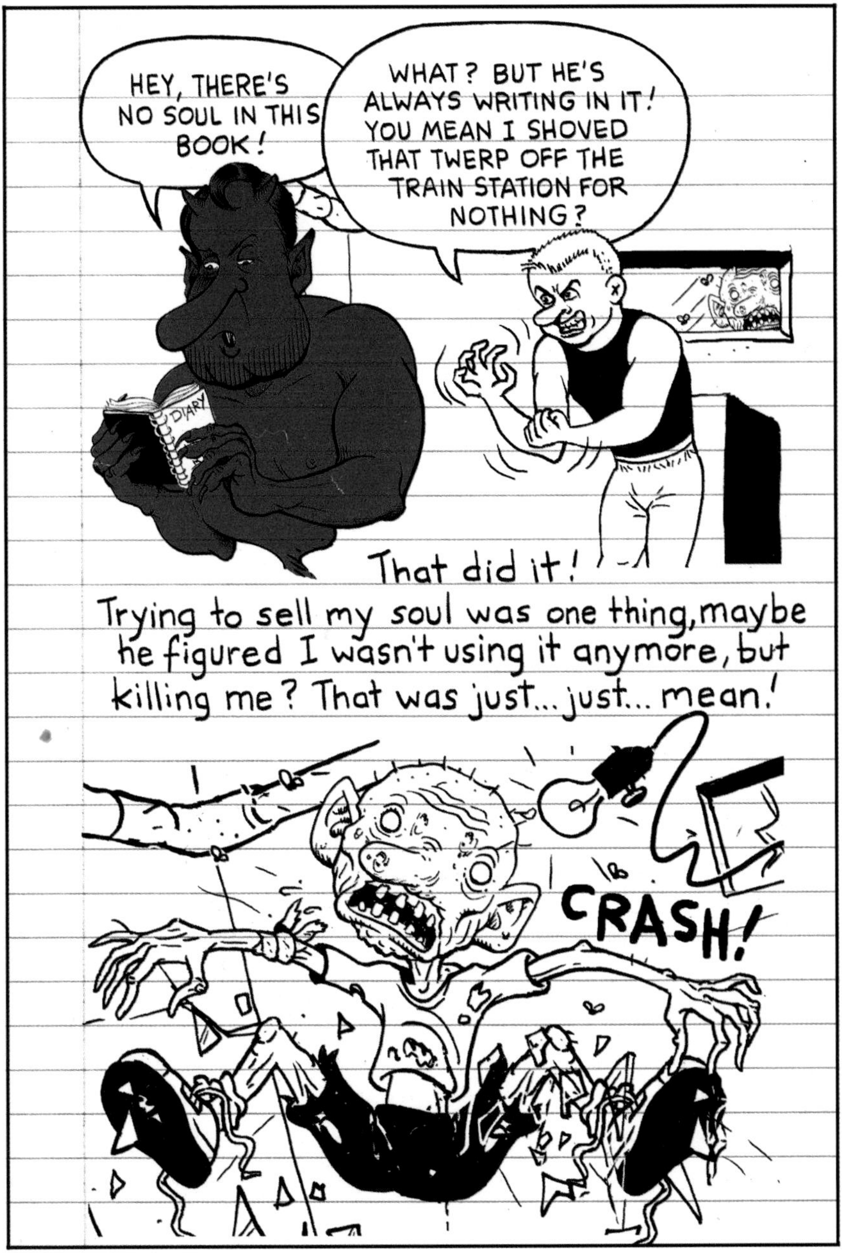
HEY, THERE'S NO SOUL IN THIS BOOK!
WHAT? BUT HE'S ALWAYS WRITING IN IT! YOU MEAN I SHOVED THAT TWERP OFF THE TRAIN STATION FOR NOTHING?
DIARY
That did it!
Trying to sell my soul was one thing, maybe he figured I wasn't using it anymore, but killing me? That was just... just... mean!
CRASH!

I told him I had it. I told him this time I wasn't going to take it anymore, I told him...

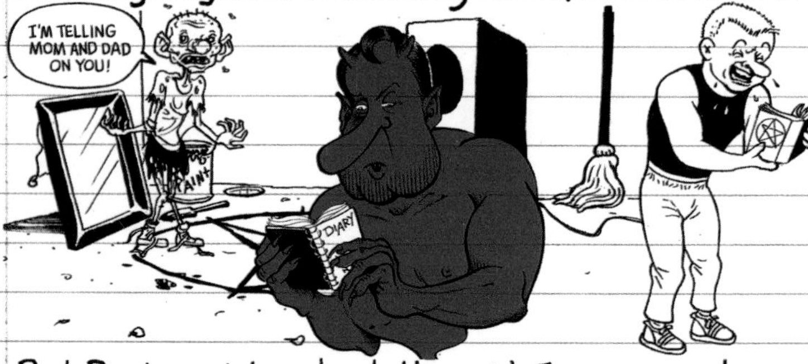
I'M TELLING MOM AND DAD ON YOU!
DIARY
PAINT

But Rock just laughed. He said I was way too much of a wuss to do anything like that, and that I smelled even worse than I used to.

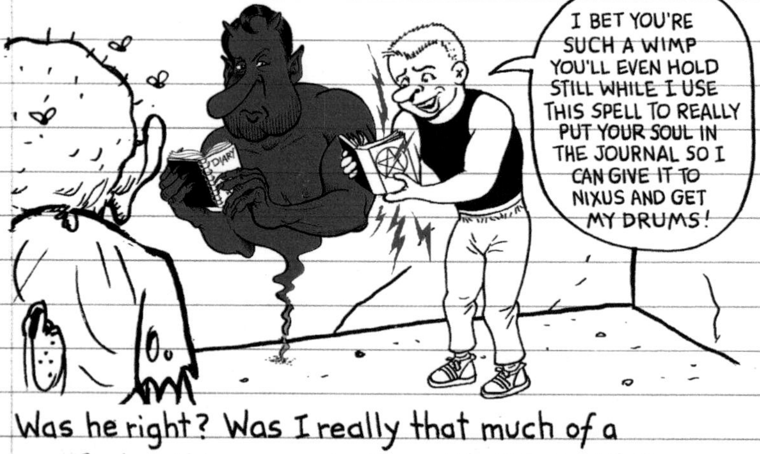
DIARY
I BET YOU'RE SUCH A WIMP YOU'LL EVEN HOLD STILL WHILE I USE THIS SPELL TO REALLY PUT YOUR SOUL IN THE JOURNAL SO I CAN GIVE IT TO NIXUS AND GET MY DRUMS!

Was he right? Was I really that much of a terrified nothing even in the afterlife? If I was going to stand up for myself, I'd have to do it soon. But what? Rock was stronger, faster and he was nearly finished with that spell.

Sad to say, he was right. I was too scared to do anything. Luckily for me, Rock had lousy aim.

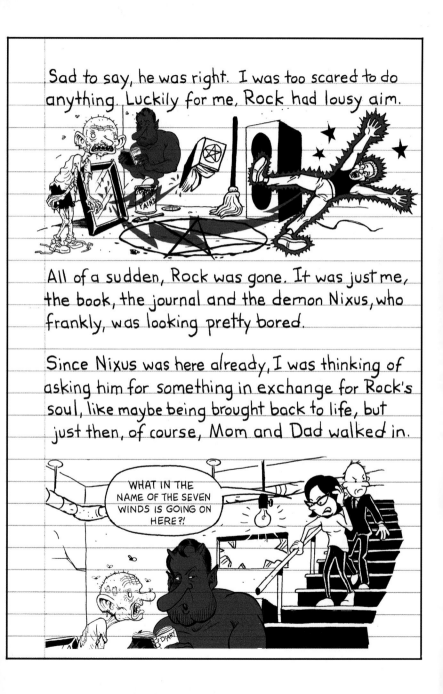

All of a sudden, Rock was gone. It was just me, the book, the journal and the demon Nixus, who frankly, was looking pretty bored.

Since Nixus was here already, I was thinking of asking him for something in exchange for Rock's soul, like maybe being brought back to life, but just then, of course, Mom and Dad walked in.

WHAT IN THE NAME OF THE SEVEN WINDS IS GOING ON HERE?!

Mom grabbed the demon Nixus by the ear and threw him out, which I didn't think was particularly fair, since the demon hadn't really done anything.

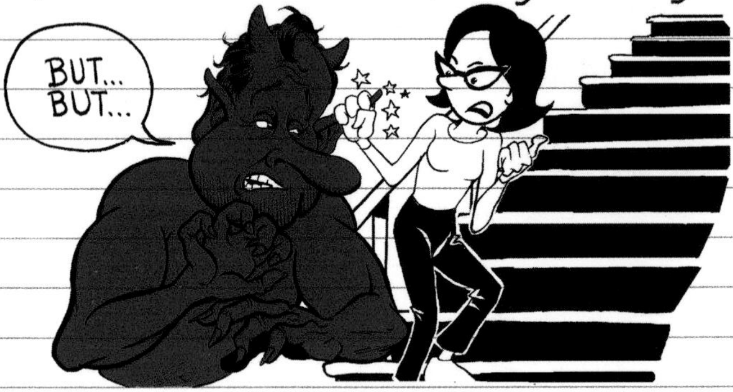
BUT... BUT...

Once he was gone, thinking quick, I "explained" that my darling brother had sacrificed himself to Nixus to bring me back, only he hadn't figured on me being a zombie.

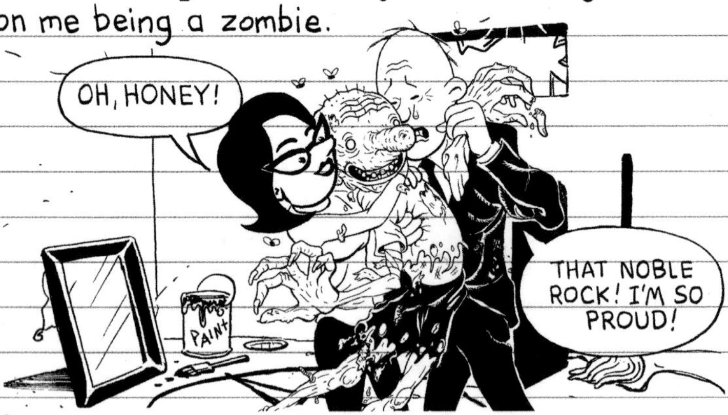
OH, HONEY!
THAT NOBLE ROCK! I'M SO PROUD!
PAINT

Guess what? They BOUGHT it! And things got better! Not that I don't still have problems.

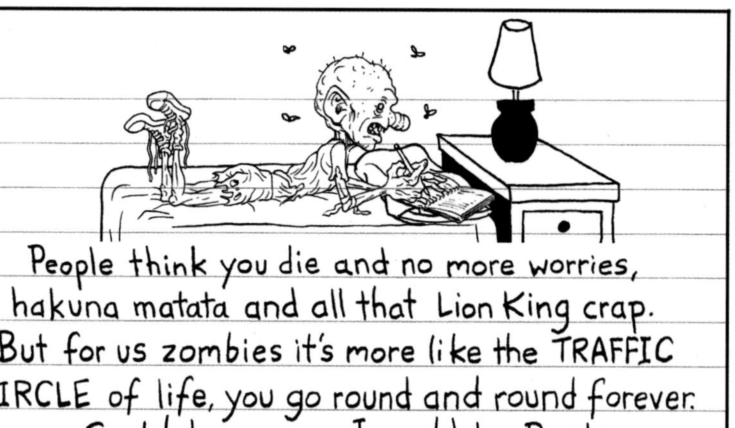

People think you die and no more worries, hakuna matata and all that Lion King crap. But for us zombies it's more like the TRAFFIC CIRCLE of life, you go round and round forever. Could be worse. I could be Rock.

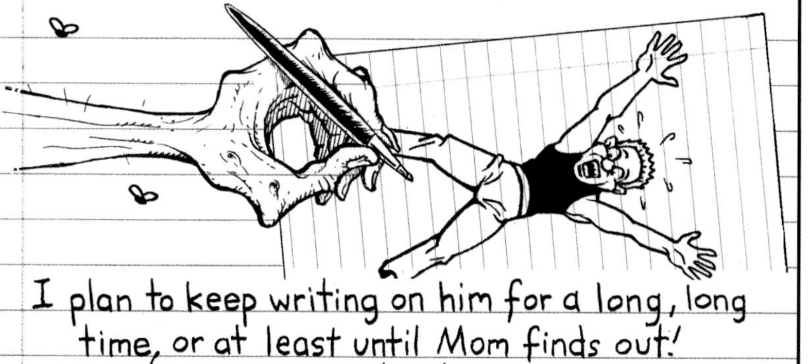

I plan to keep writing on him for a long, long time, or at least until Mom finds out!

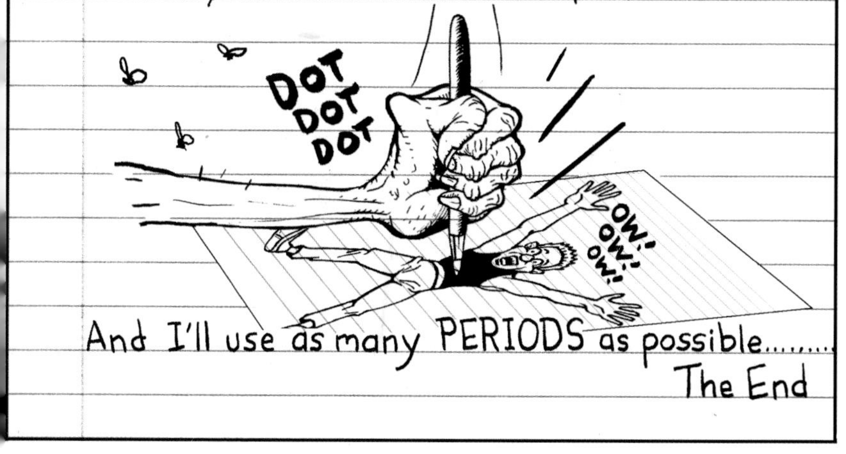
DOT
DOT
DOT
OW!
OW!
OW!

And I'll use as many PERIODS as possible........

The End

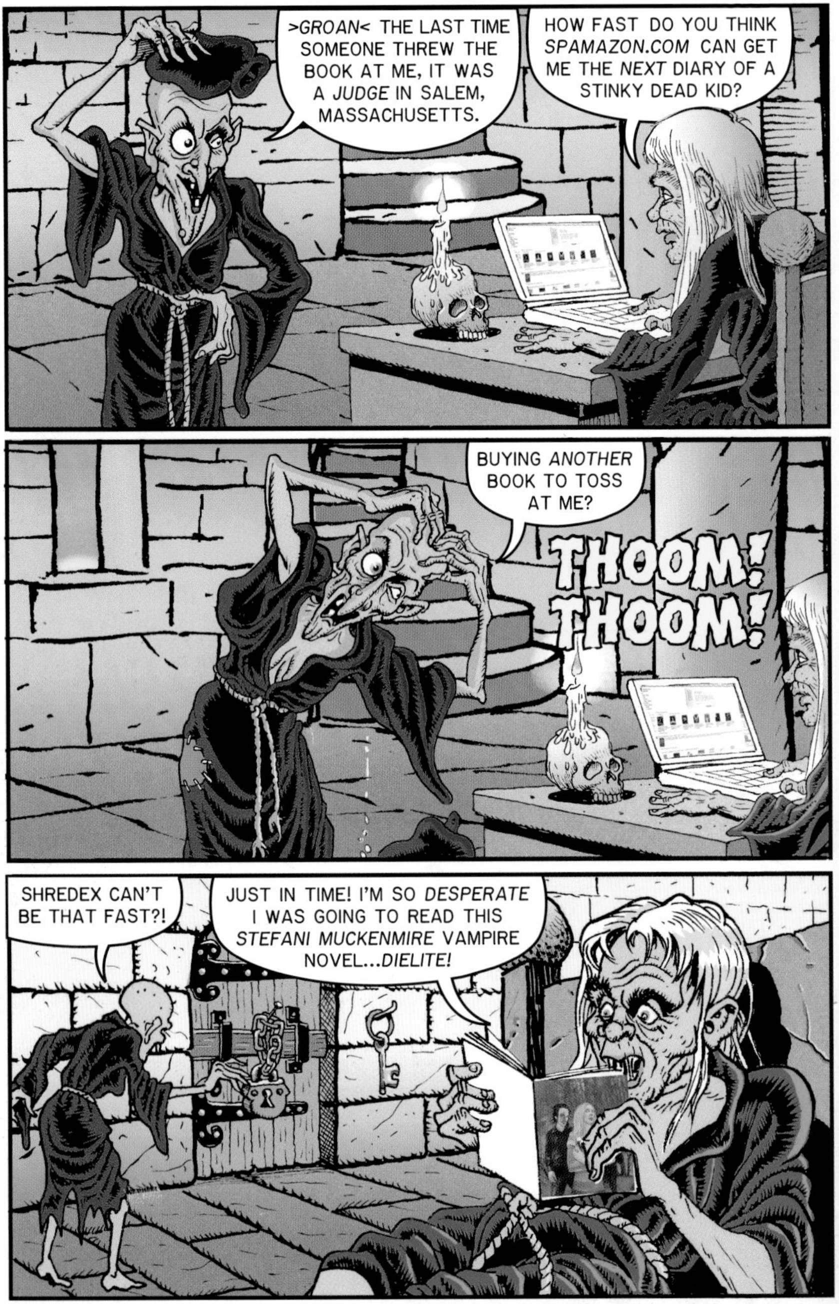
>*GROAN*< THE LAST TIME SOMEONE THREW THE BOOK AT ME, IT WAS A *JUDGE* IN SALEM, MASSACHUSETTS.
HOW FAST DO YOU THINK *SPAMAZON.COM* CAN GET ME THE *NEXT* DIARY OF A STINKY DEAD KID?
BUYING *ANOTHER* BOOK TO TOSS AT ME?
THOOM! THOOM!
SHREDEX CAN'T BE THAT FAST?!
JUST IN TIME! I'M SO *DESPERATE* I WAS GOING TO READ THIS *STEFANI MUCKENMIRE* VAMPIRE NOVEL...*DIELITE!*

My name is **Lou Anne Lugosi**. I was sent off to live in the little town of Sporks because my mother totally hated me. Now I'm stuck in this dismal dump living with my clueless father.
It was my first day of school, and of course I didn't get my hopes up. I knew from the beginning my life in Sporks would suck.
But I didn't realize that meant **literally**.
음료수
As I walked self-consciously to a table at lunch, I felt like someone was **watching**.

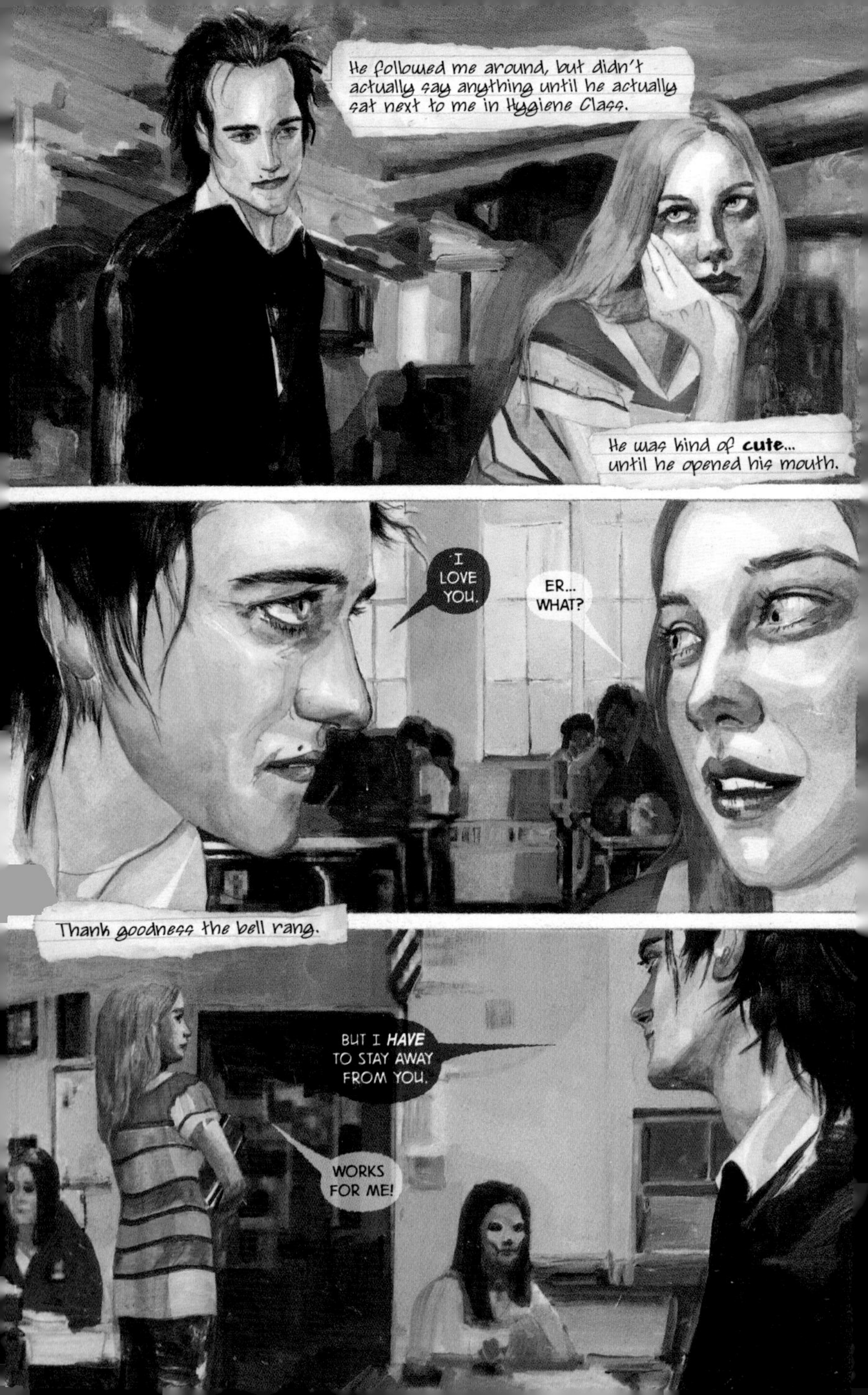
He followed me around, but didn't actually say anything until he actually sat next to me in Hygiene Class.
He was kind of **cute**... until he opened his mouth.
I LOVE YOU.
ER... WHAT?
Thank goodness the bell rang.
BUT I *HAVE* TO STAY AWAY FROM YOU.
WORKS FOR ME!

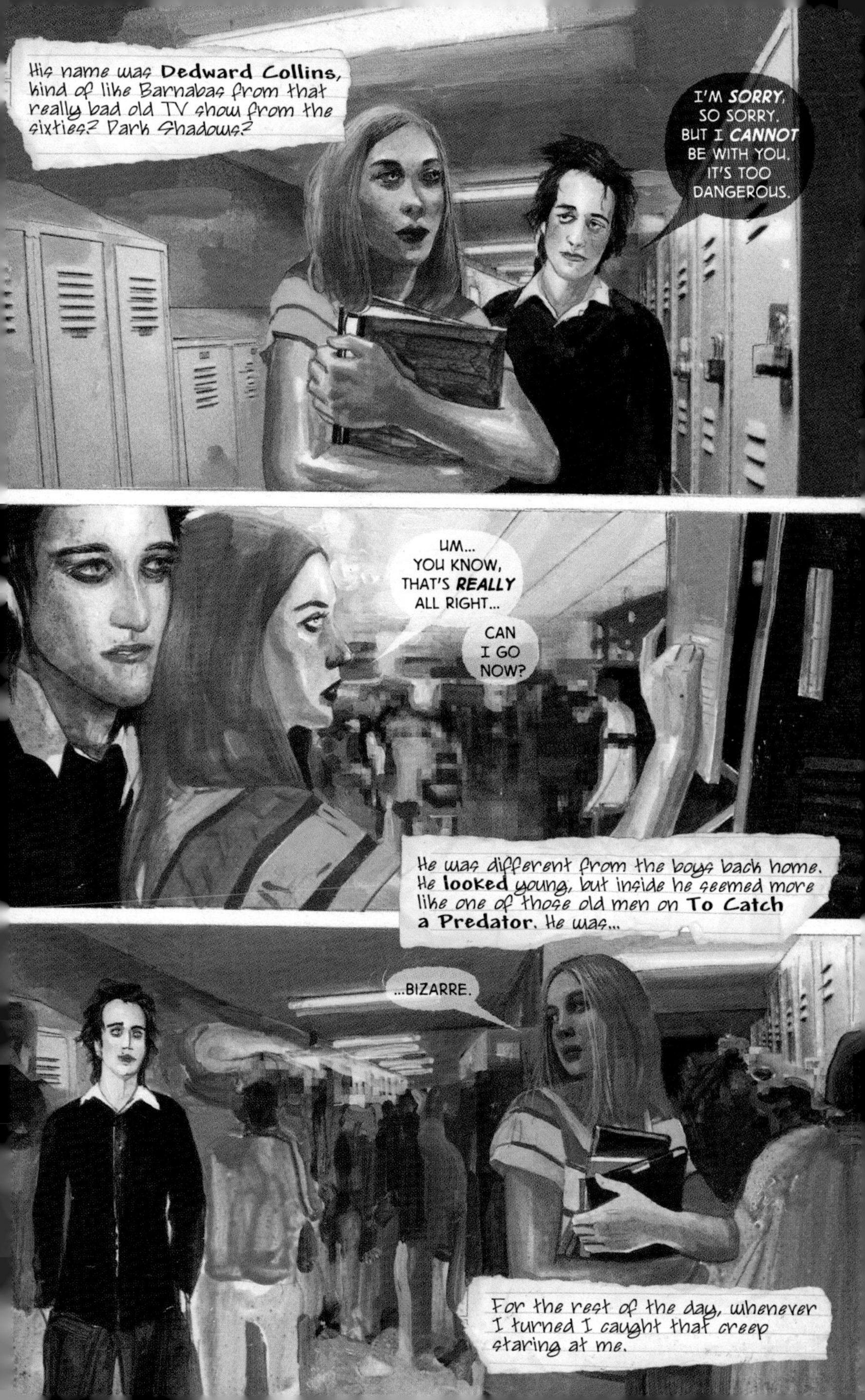
His name was Dedward Collins, kind of like Barnabas from that really bad old TV show from the sixties? Dark Shadows?
I'M SORRY, SO SORRY. BUT I CANNOT BE WITH YOU. IT'S TOO DANGEROUS.
UM... YOU KNOW, THAT'S REALLY ALL RIGHT...
CAN I GO NOW?
He was different from the boys back home. He looked young, but inside he seemed more like one of those old men on To Catch a Predator. He was...
...BIZARRE.
For the rest of the day, whenever I turned I caught that creep staring at me.

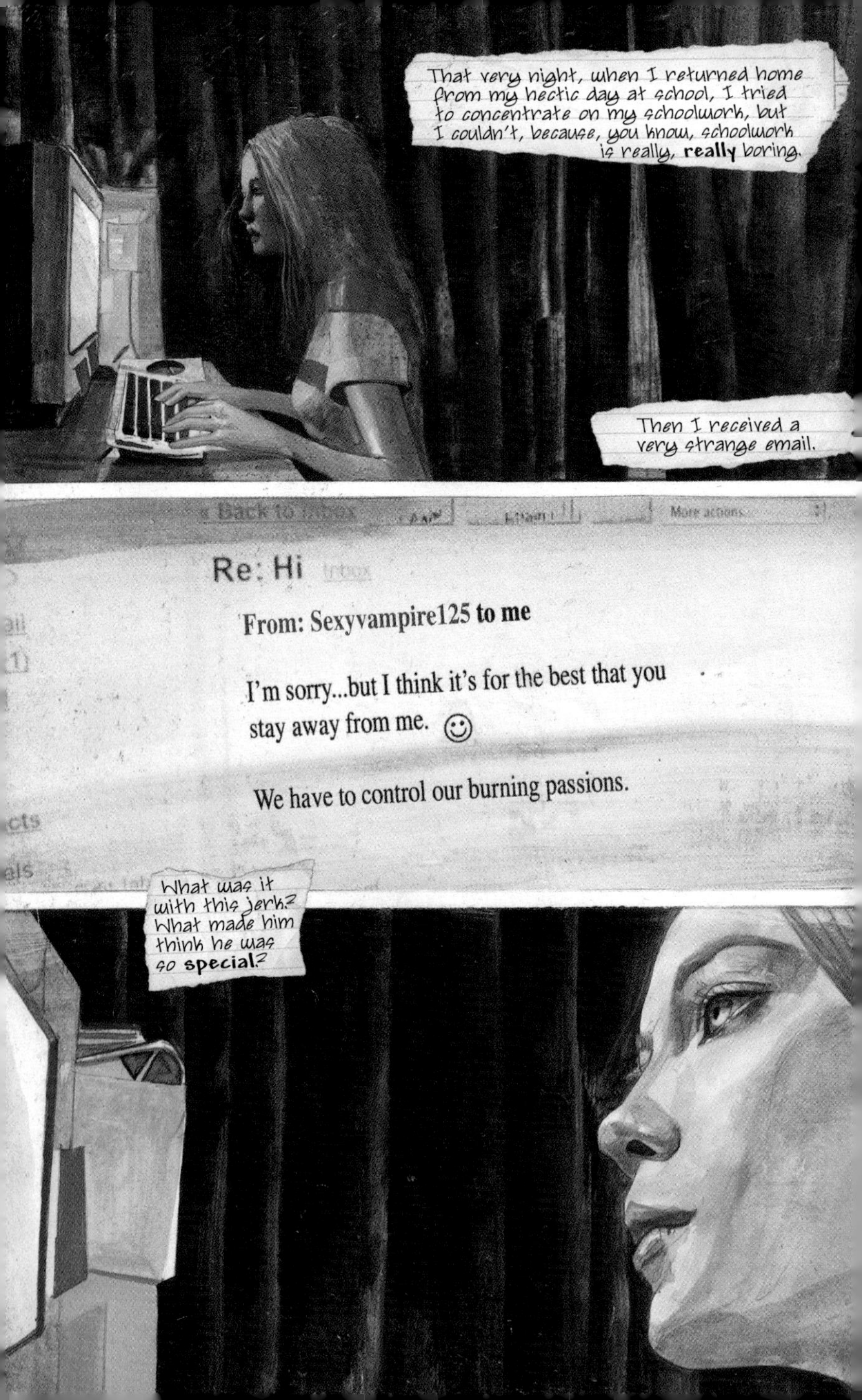

That very night, when I returned home from my hectic day at school, I tried to concentrate on my schoolwork, but I couldn't, because, you know, schoolwork is really, **really** boring.
Then I received a very strange email.
More actions
Re: Hi
From: Sexyvampire125 to me
I'm sorry...but I think it's for the best that you stay away from me. ☺
We have to control our burning passions.
What was it with this jerk? What made him think he was so **special**?

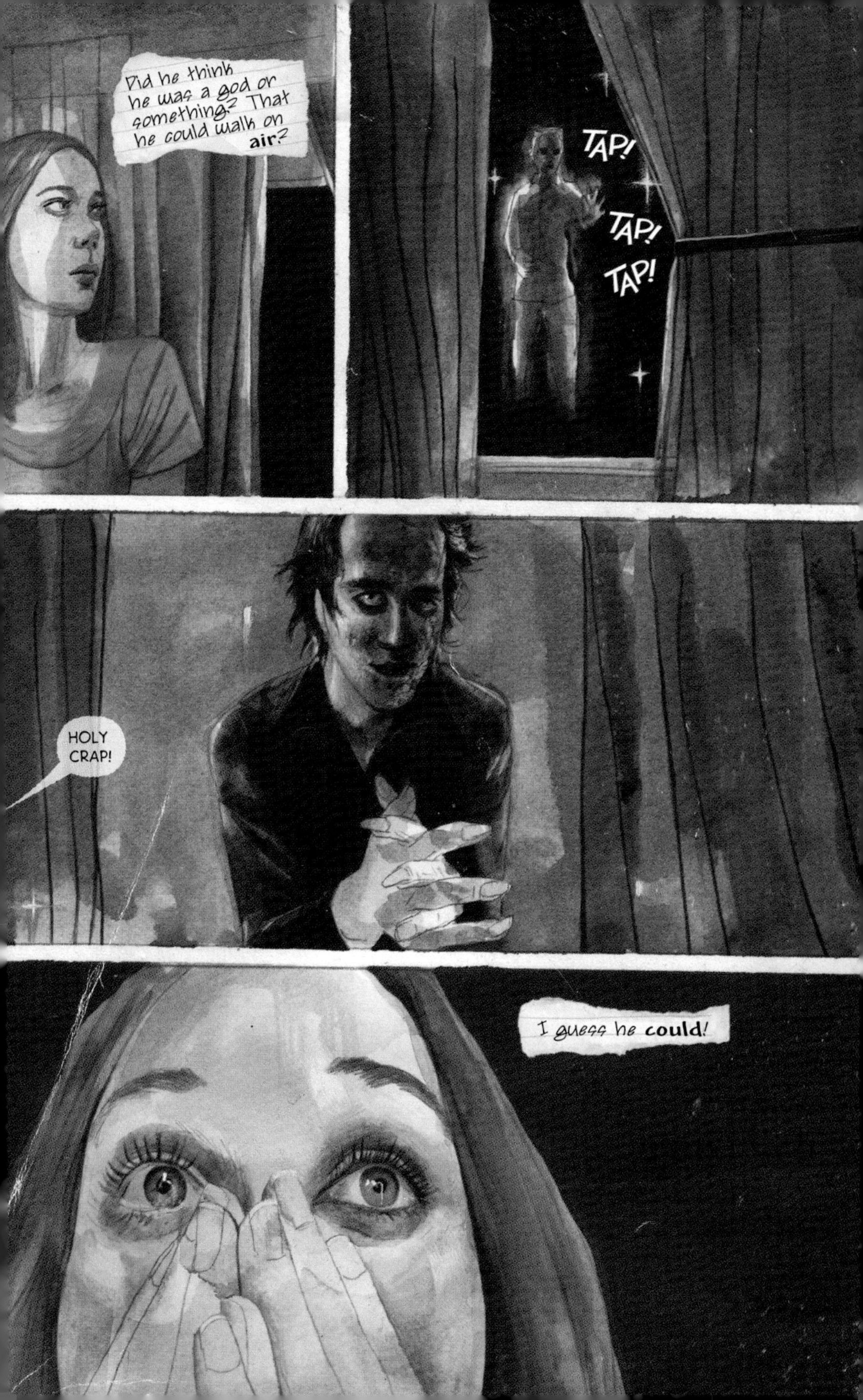
Did he think he was a god or something? That he could walk on air?
TAP!
TAP!
TAP!
HOLY CRAP!
I guess he could!

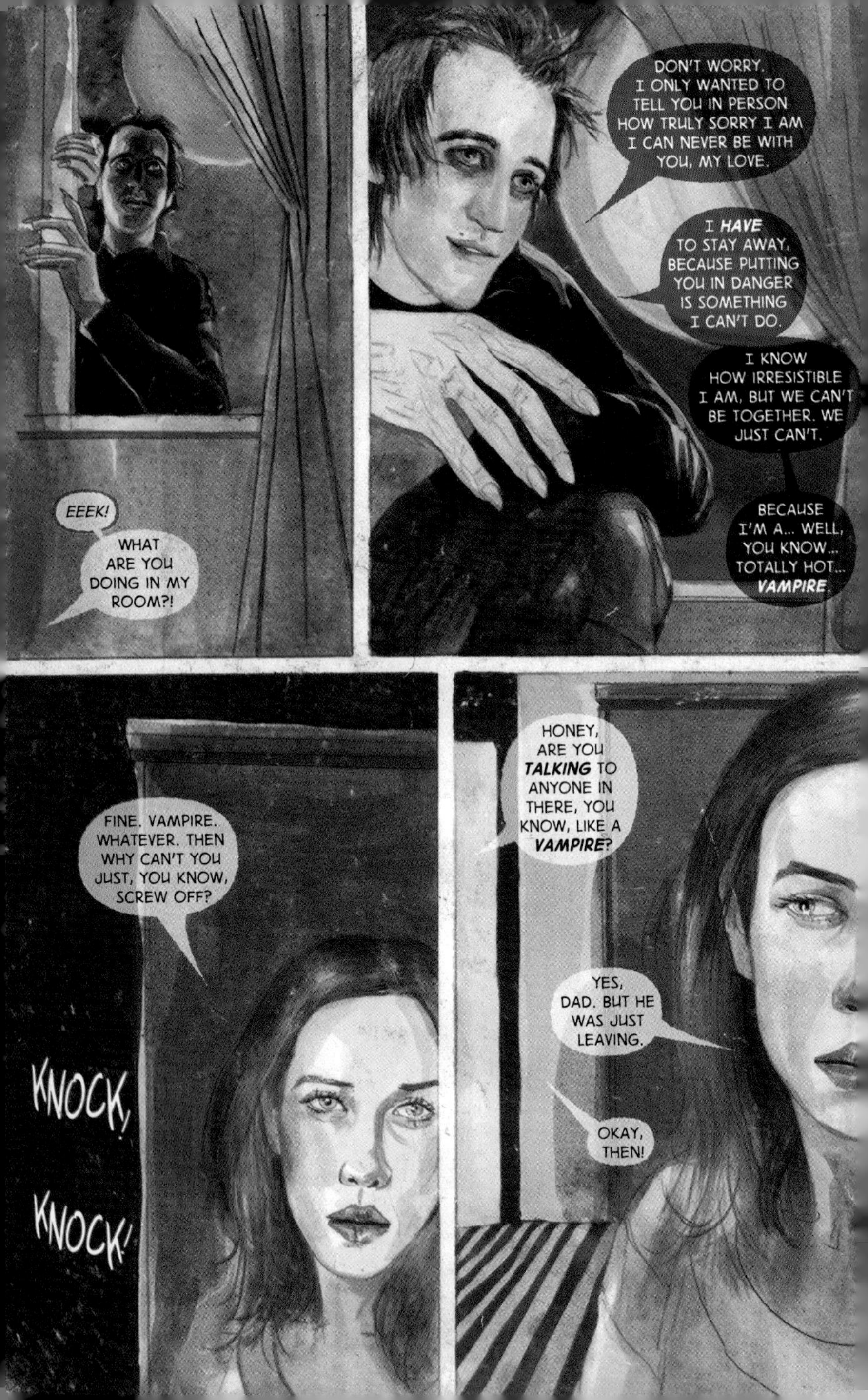
EEEK!
WHAT ARE YOU DOING IN MY ROOM?!
DON'T WORRY. I ONLY WANTED TO TELL YOU IN PERSON HOW TRULY SORRY I AM I CAN NEVER BE WITH YOU, MY LOVE.
I HAVE TO STAY AWAY, BECAUSE PUTTING YOU IN DANGER IS SOMETHING I CAN'T DO.
I KNOW HOW IRRESISTIBLE I AM, BUT WE CAN'T BE TOGETHER. WE JUST CAN'T.
BECAUSE I'M A... WELL, YOU KNOW... TOTALLY HOT... VAMPIRE.
FINE. VAMPIRE. WHATEVER. THEN WHY CAN'T YOU JUST, YOU KNOW, SCREW OFF?
KNOCK, KNOCK!
HONEY, ARE YOU TALKING TO ANYONE IN THERE, YOU KNOW, LIKE A VAMPIRE?
YES, DAD. BUT HE WAS JUST LEAVING.
OKAY, THEN!

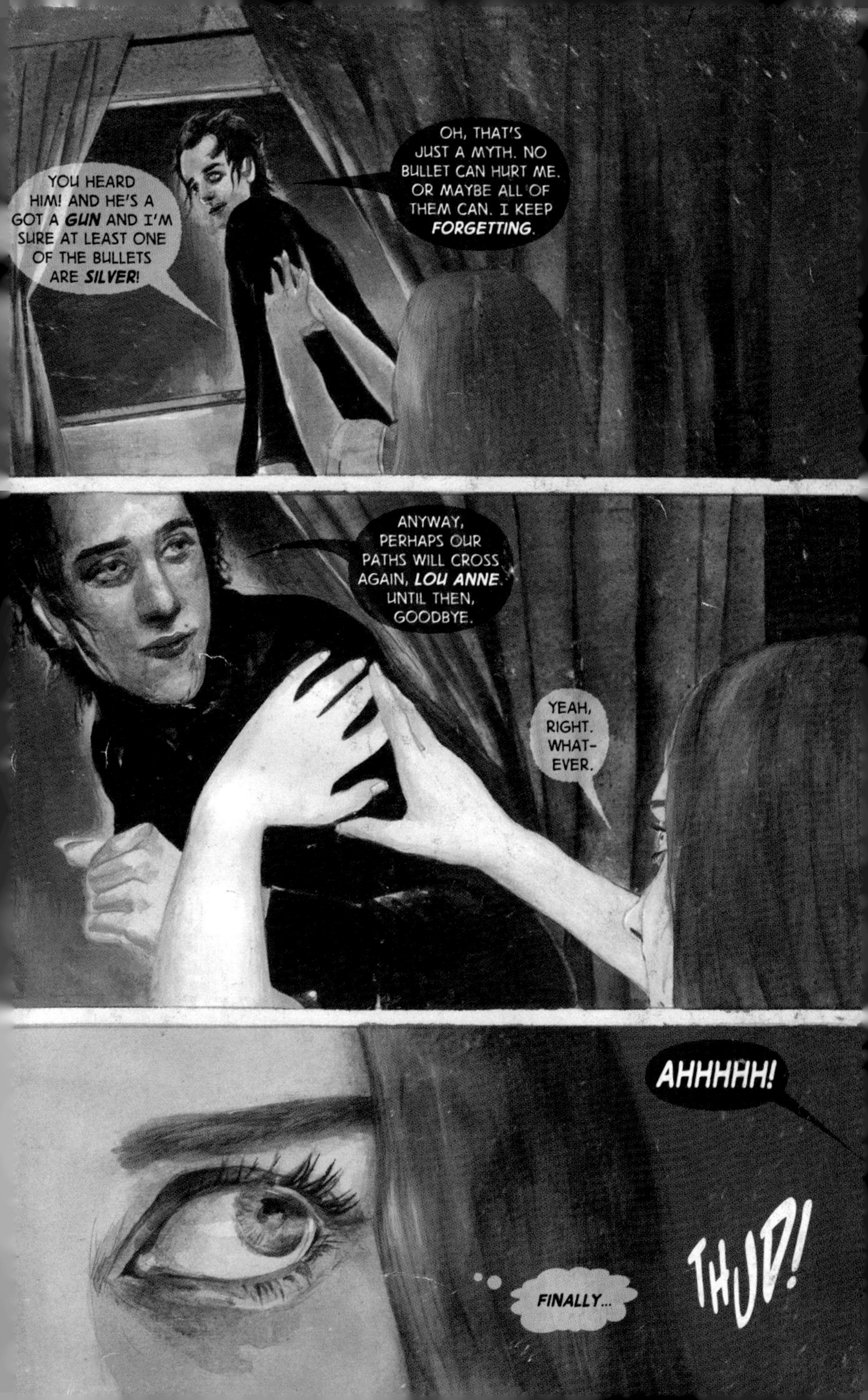
YOU HEARD HIM! AND HE'S A GOT A GUN AND I'M SURE AT LEAST ONE OF THE BULLETS ARE SILVER!
OH, THAT'S JUST A MYTH. NO BULLET CAN HURT ME. OR MAYBE ALL OF THEM CAN. I KEEP FORGETTING.
ANYWAY, PERHAPS OUR PATHS WILL CROSS AGAIN, LOU ANNE. UNTIL THEN, GOODBYE.
YEAH, RIGHT. WHAT-EVER.
AHHHHH!
FINALLY...
THUD!

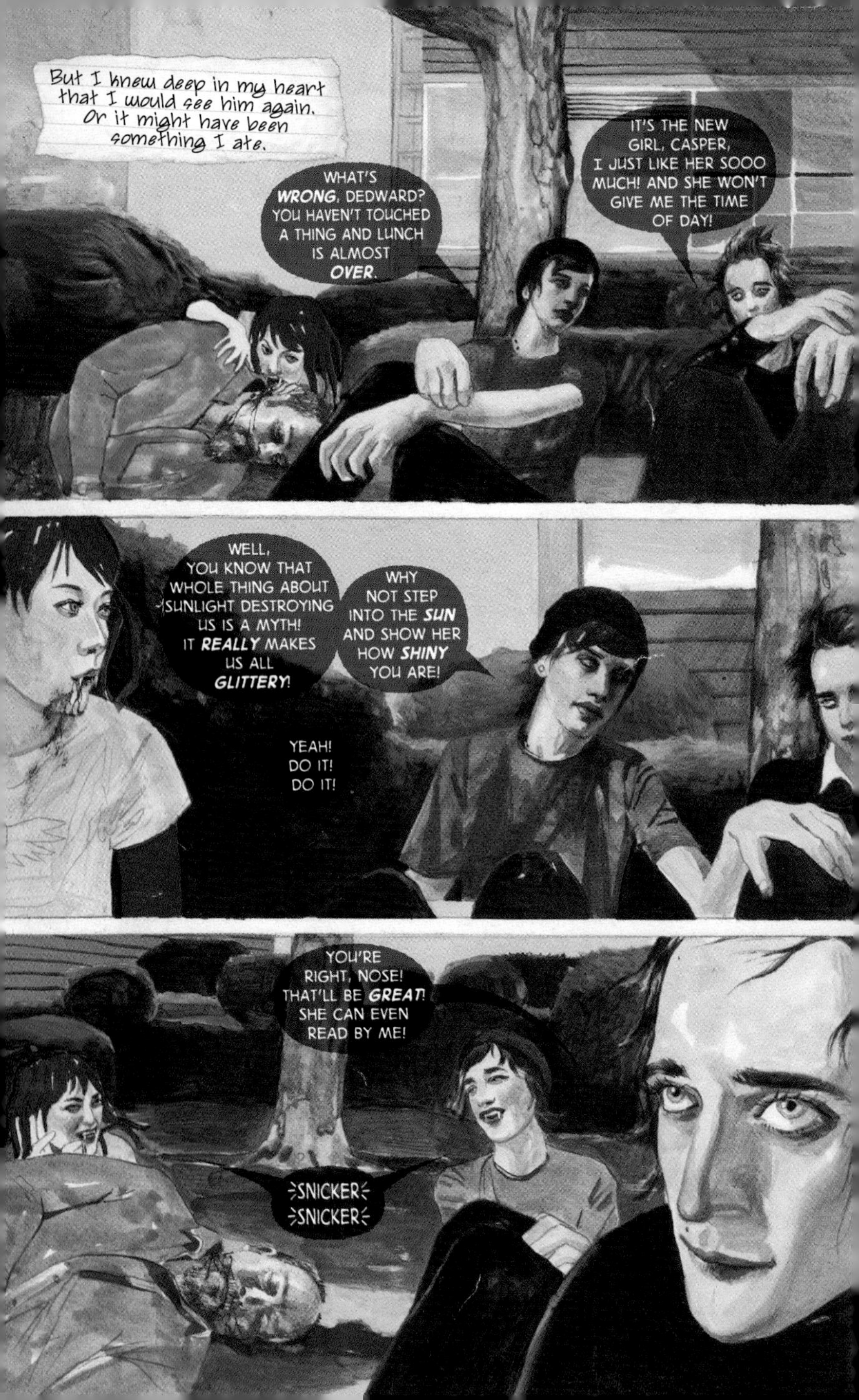
But I knew deep in my heart that I would see him again. Or it might have been something I ate.
WHAT'S WRONG, DEDWARD? YOU HAVEN'T TOUCHED A THING AND LUNCH IS ALMOST OVER.
IT'S THE NEW GIRL, CASPER, I JUST LIKE HER SOOO MUCH! AND SHE WON'T GIVE ME THE TIME OF DAY!
WELL, YOU KNOW THAT WHOLE THING ABOUT SUNLIGHT DESTROYING US IS A MYTH! IT REALLY MAKES US ALL GLITTERY!
WHY NOT STEP INTO THE SUN AND SHOW HER HOW SHINY YOU ARE!
YEAH! DO IT! DO IT!
YOU'RE RIGHT, NOSE! THAT'LL BE GREAT! SHE CAN EVEN READ BY ME!
SNICKER SNICKER

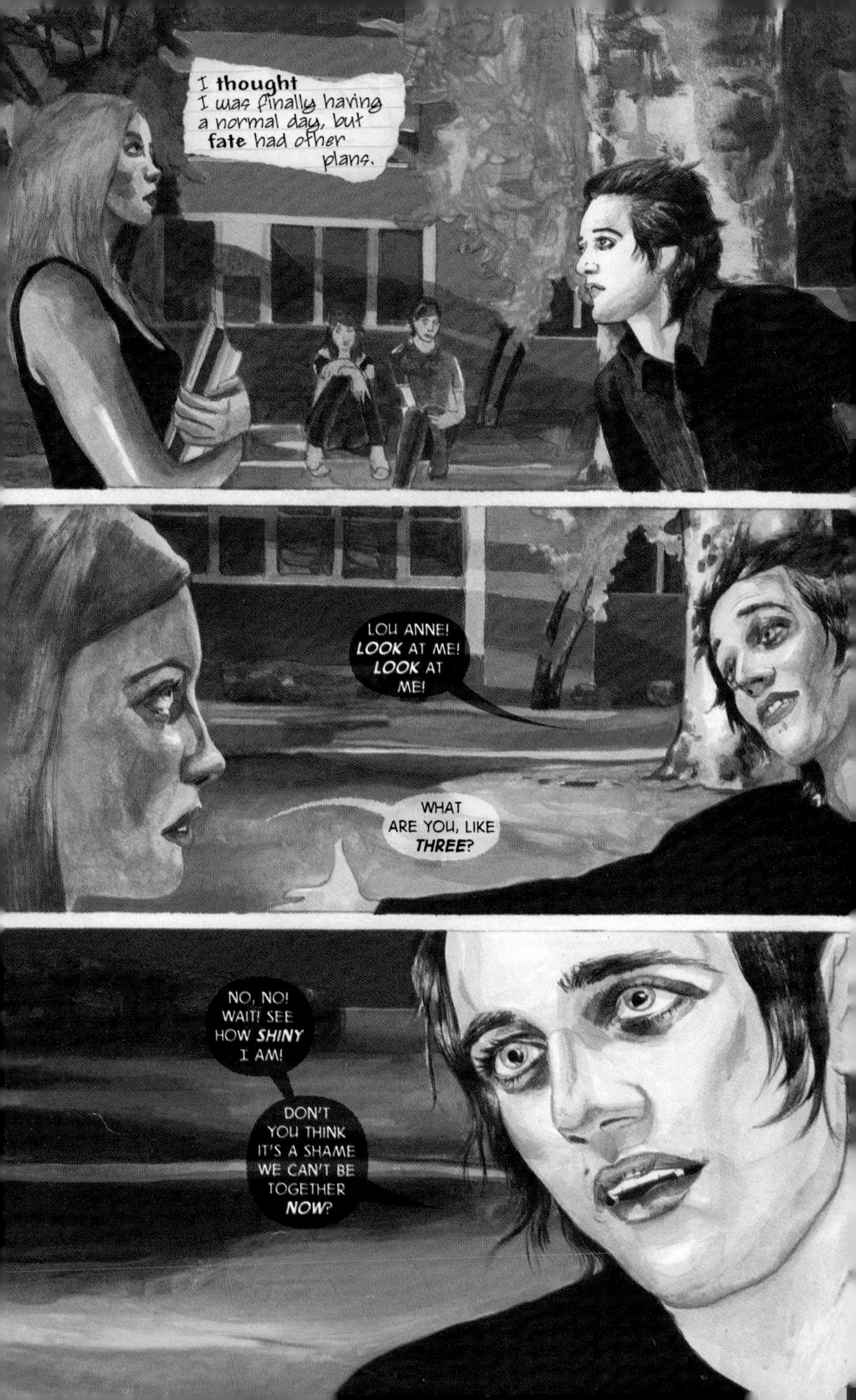
I thought I was finally having a normal day, but fate had other plans.
LOU ANNE! LOOK AT ME! LOOK AT ME!
WHAT ARE YOU, LIKE THREE?
NO, NO! WAIT! SEE HOW SHINY I AM!
DON'T YOU THINK IT'S A SHAME WE CAN'T BE TOGETHER NOW?

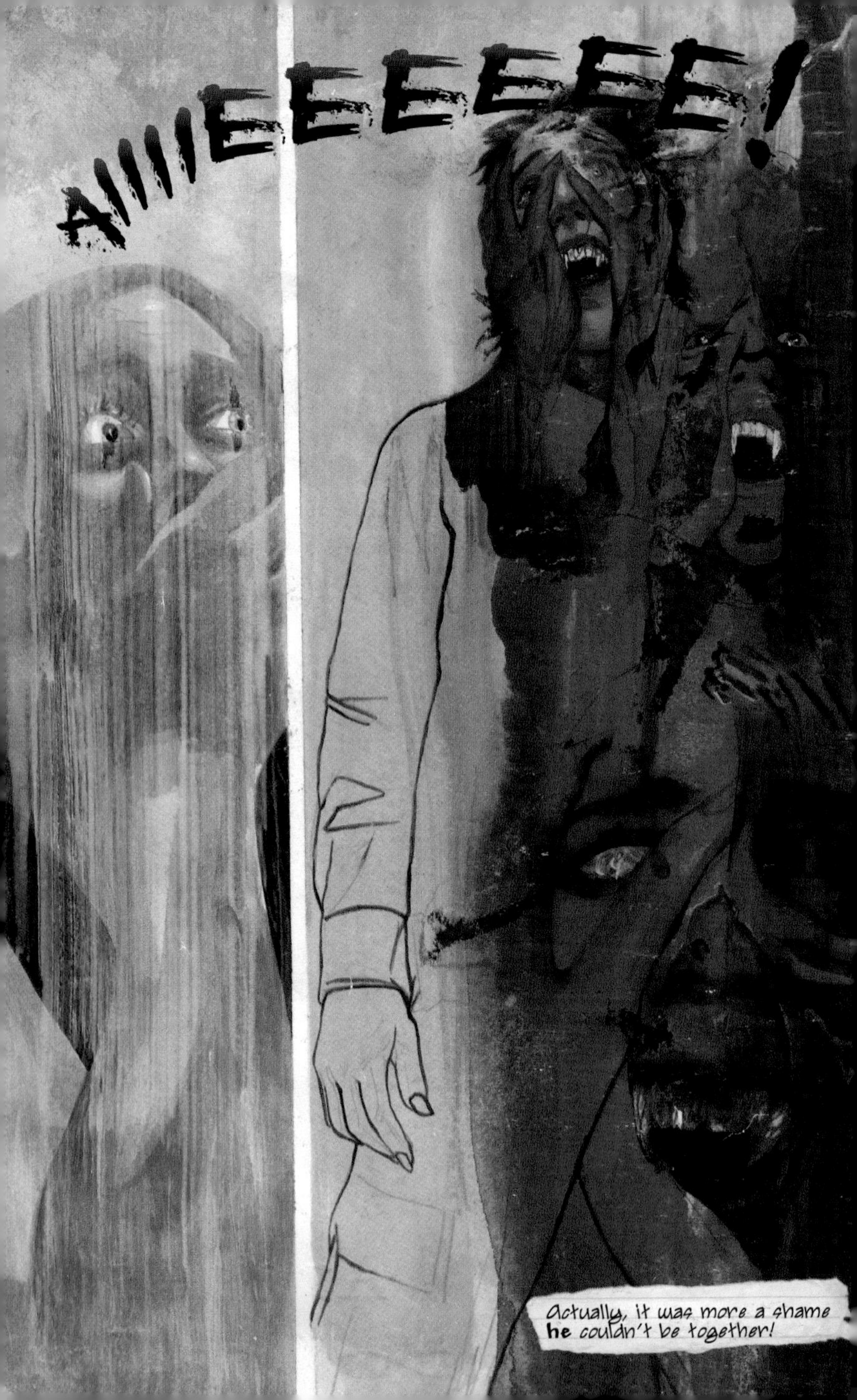
AIIIIEEEEEEE!
Actually, it was more a shame
he couldn't be together!

YEAH, SMELLING LIKE BURNT HAMBURGER HAS ALWAYS BEEN A BIG TURN ON FOR ME, **LOSER**!
YIE! YIE! YIE!
HEE-HEE! DID YOU SEE THE LOOK ON HIS FACE?
More vampires? My first thought was that I should change schools. Maybe to one not so monster infested...
WHY? DID IT **FALL OFF?** AH -HA-HA-HA!
Then again, maybe they could be **useful**.

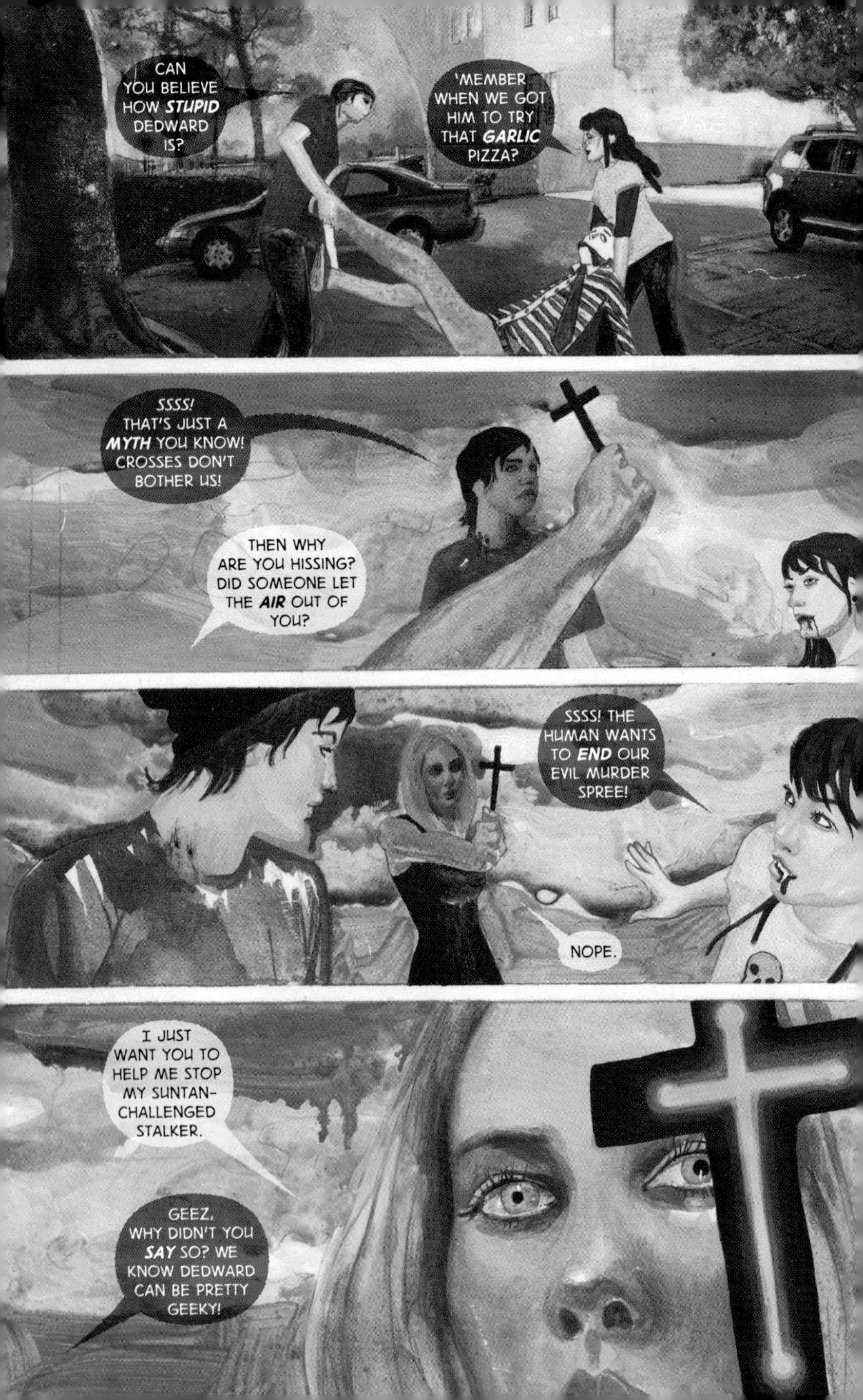
CAN YOU BELIEVE HOW STUPID DEDWARD IS?
'MEMBER WHEN WE GOT HIM TO TRY THAT GARLIC PIZZA?
SSSS! THAT'S JUST A MYTH YOU KNOW! CROSSES DON'T BOTHER US!
THEN WHY ARE YOU HISSING? DID SOMEONE LET THE AIR OUT OF YOU?
SSSS! THE HUMAN WANTS TO END OUR EVIL MURDER SPREE!
NOPE.
I JUST WANT YOU TO HELP ME STOP MY SUNTAN-CHALLENGED STALKER.
GEEZ, WHY DIDN'T YOU SAY SO? WE KNOW DEDWARD CAN BE PRETTY GEEKY!

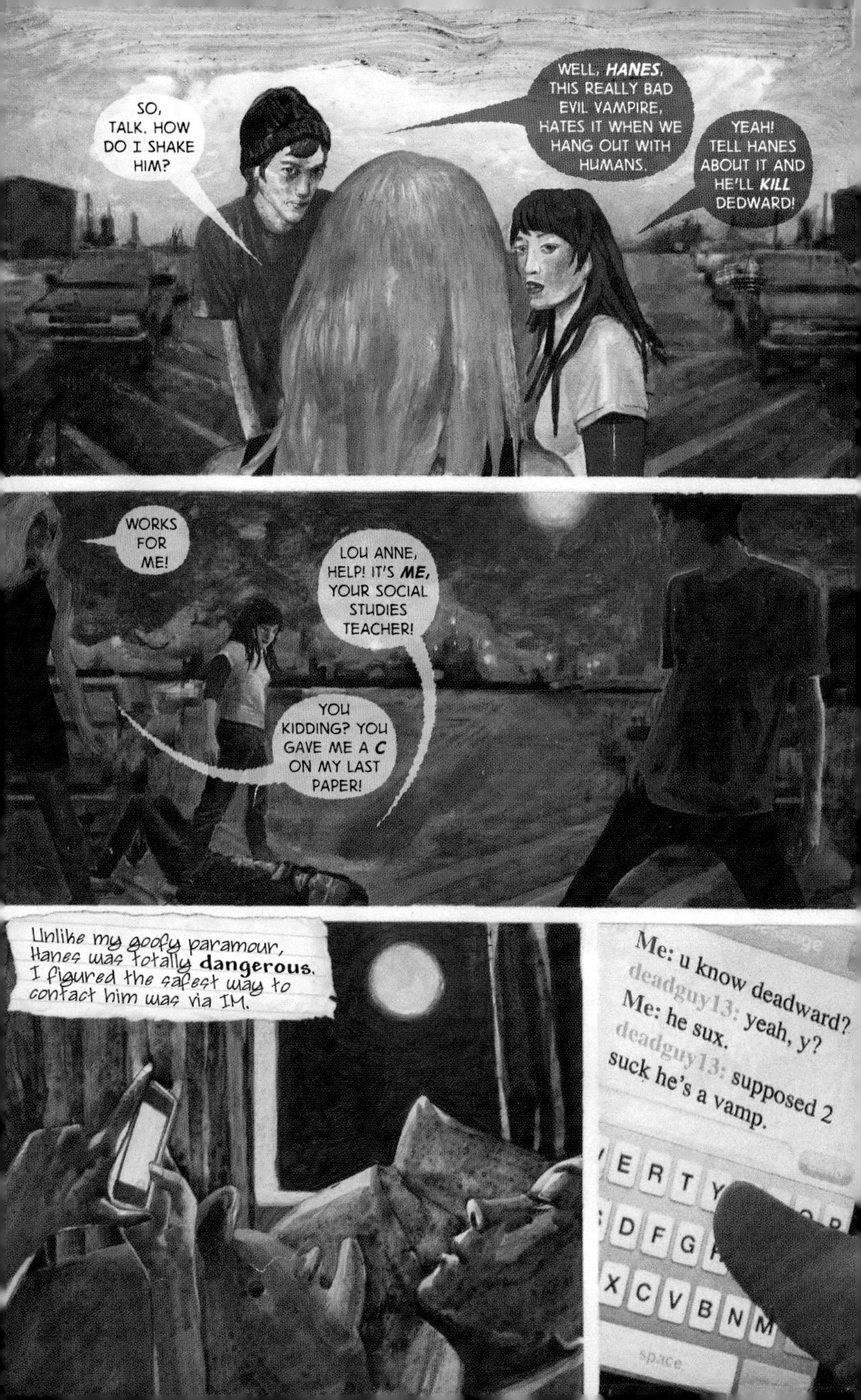
SO, TALK. HOW DO I SHAKE HIM?
WELL, HANES, THIS REALLY BAD EVIL VAMPIRE, HATES IT WHEN WE HANG OUT WITH HUMANS.
YEAH! TELL HANES ABOUT IT AND HE'LL KILL DEDWARD!
WORKS FOR ME!
LOU ANNE, HELP! IT'S ME, YOUR SOCIAL STUDIES TEACHER!
YOU KIDDING? YOU GAVE ME A C ON MY LAST PAPER!
Unlike my goofy paramour, Hanes was totally dangerous. I figured the safest way to contact him was via IM.
Me: u know deadward?
deadguy13: yeah, y?
Me: he sux.
deadguy13: supposed 2 suck he's a vamp.

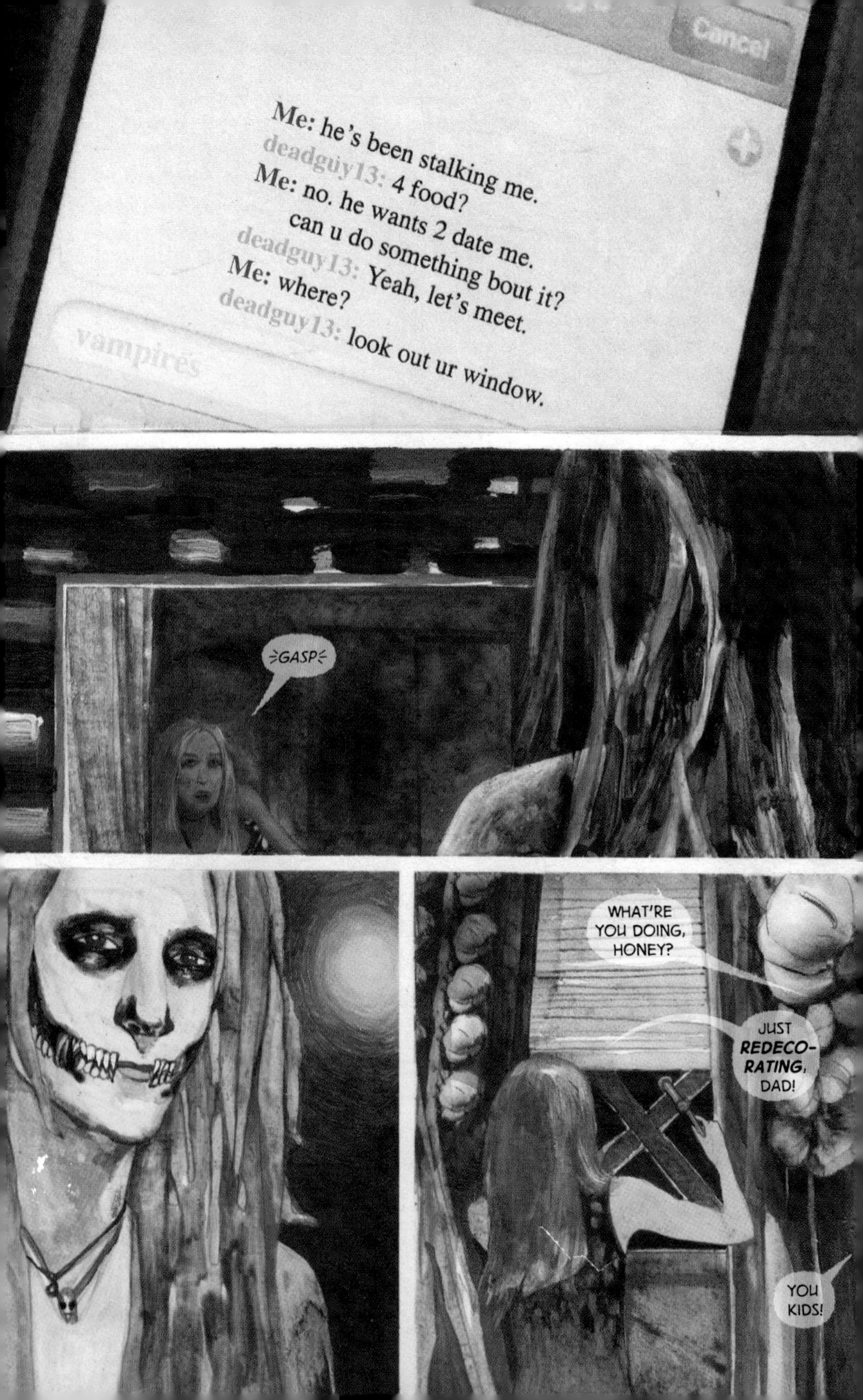

Cancel
Me: he's been stalking me.
deadguy13: 4 food?
Me: no. he wants 2 date me.
can u do something bout it?
deadguy13: Yeah, let's meet.
Me: where?
deadguy13: look out ur window.
vampires
GASP
WHAT'RE YOU DOING, HONEY?
JUST REDECO-RATING, DAD!
YOU KIDS!

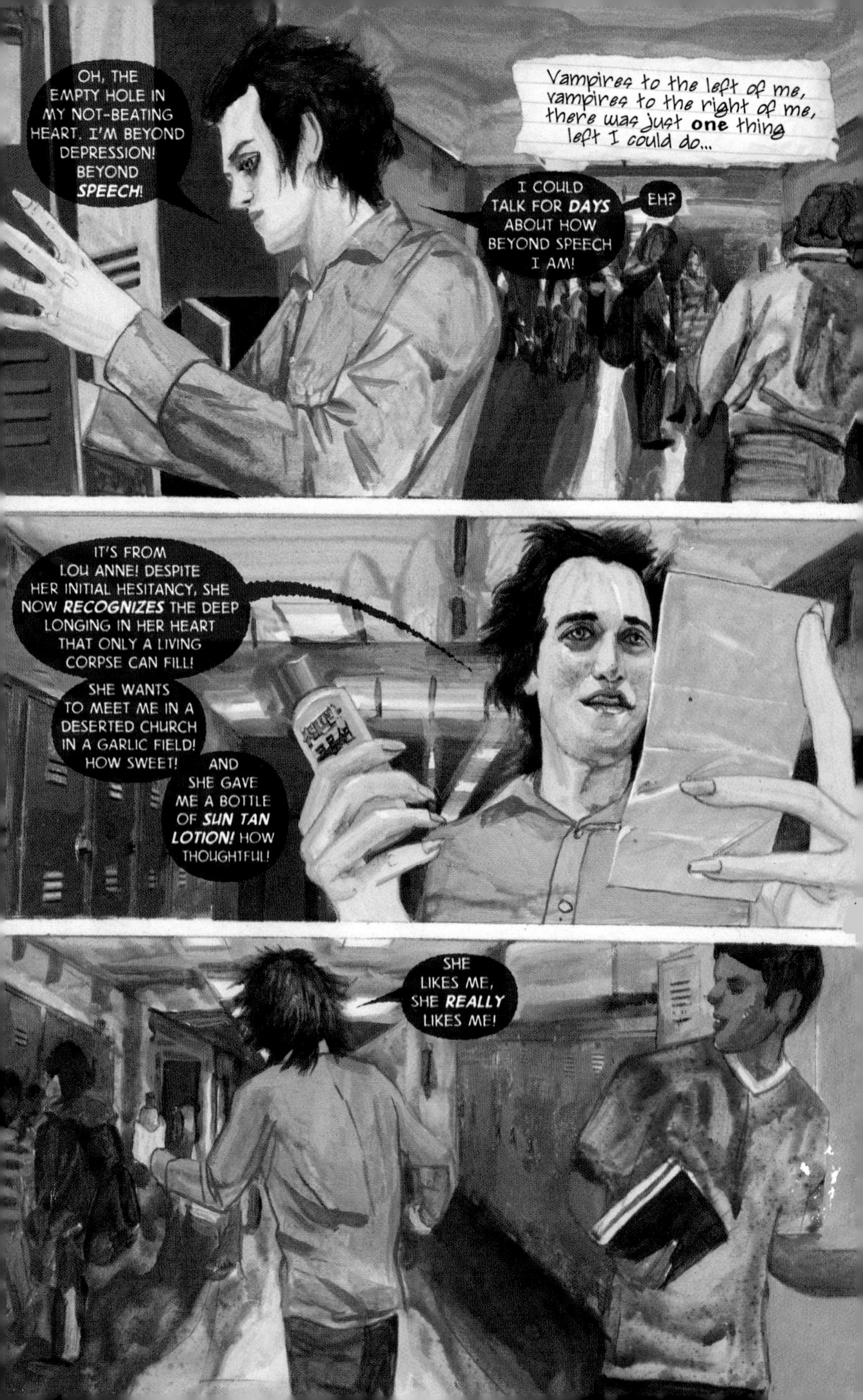
OH, THE EMPTY HOLE IN MY NOT-BEATING HEART. I'M BEYOND DEPRESSION! BEYOND SPEECH!
Vampires to the left of me, vampires to the right of me, there was just one thing left I could do...
I COULD TALK FOR DAYS ABOUT HOW BEYOND SPEECH I AM!
EH?
IT'S FROM LOU ANNE! DESPITE HER INITIAL HESITANCY, SHE NOW RECOGNIZES THE DEEP LONGING IN HER HEART THAT ONLY A LIVING CORPSE CAN FILL!
SHE WANTS TO MEET ME IN A DESERTED CHURCH IN A GARLIC FIELD! HOW SWEET!
AND SHE GAVE ME A BOTTLE OF SUN TAN LOTION! HOW THOUGHTFUL!
SHE LIKES ME, SHE REALLY LIKES ME!

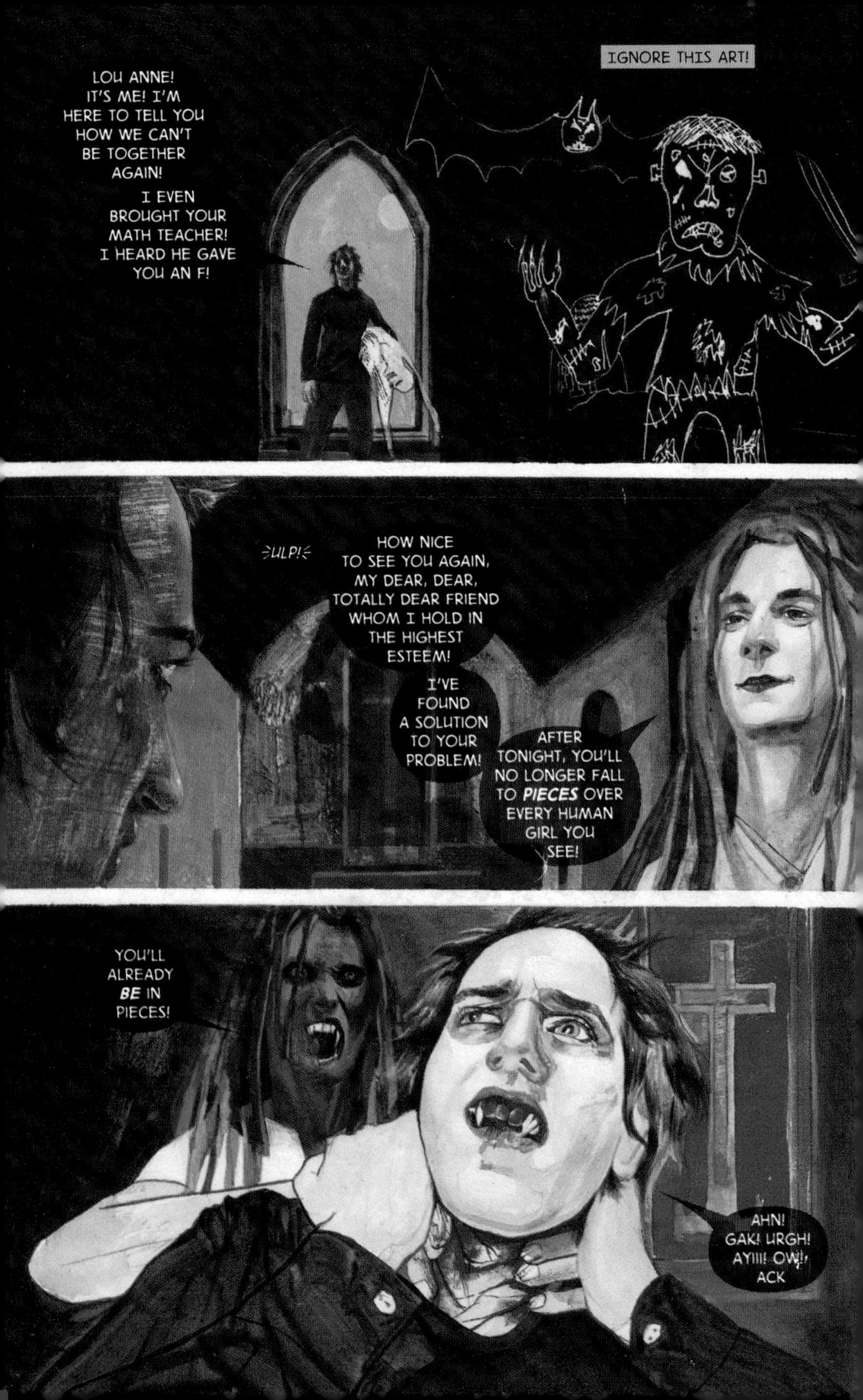
IGNORE THIS ART!
LOU ANNE! IT'S ME! I'M HERE TO TELL YOU HOW WE CAN'T BE TOGETHER AGAIN!
I EVEN BROUGHT YOUR MATH TEACHER! I HEARD HE GAVE YOU AN F!
ULP!
HOW NICE TO SEE YOU AGAIN, MY DEAR, DEAR, TOTALLY DEAR FRIEND WHOM I HOLD IN THE HIGHEST ESTEEM!
I'VE FOUND A SOLUTION TO YOUR PROBLEM!
AFTER TONIGHT, YOU'LL NO LONGER FALL TO PIECES OVER EVERY HUMAN GIRL YOU SEE!
YOU'LL ALREADY BE IN PIECES!
AHN! GAK! URGH! AYIII! OW! ACK

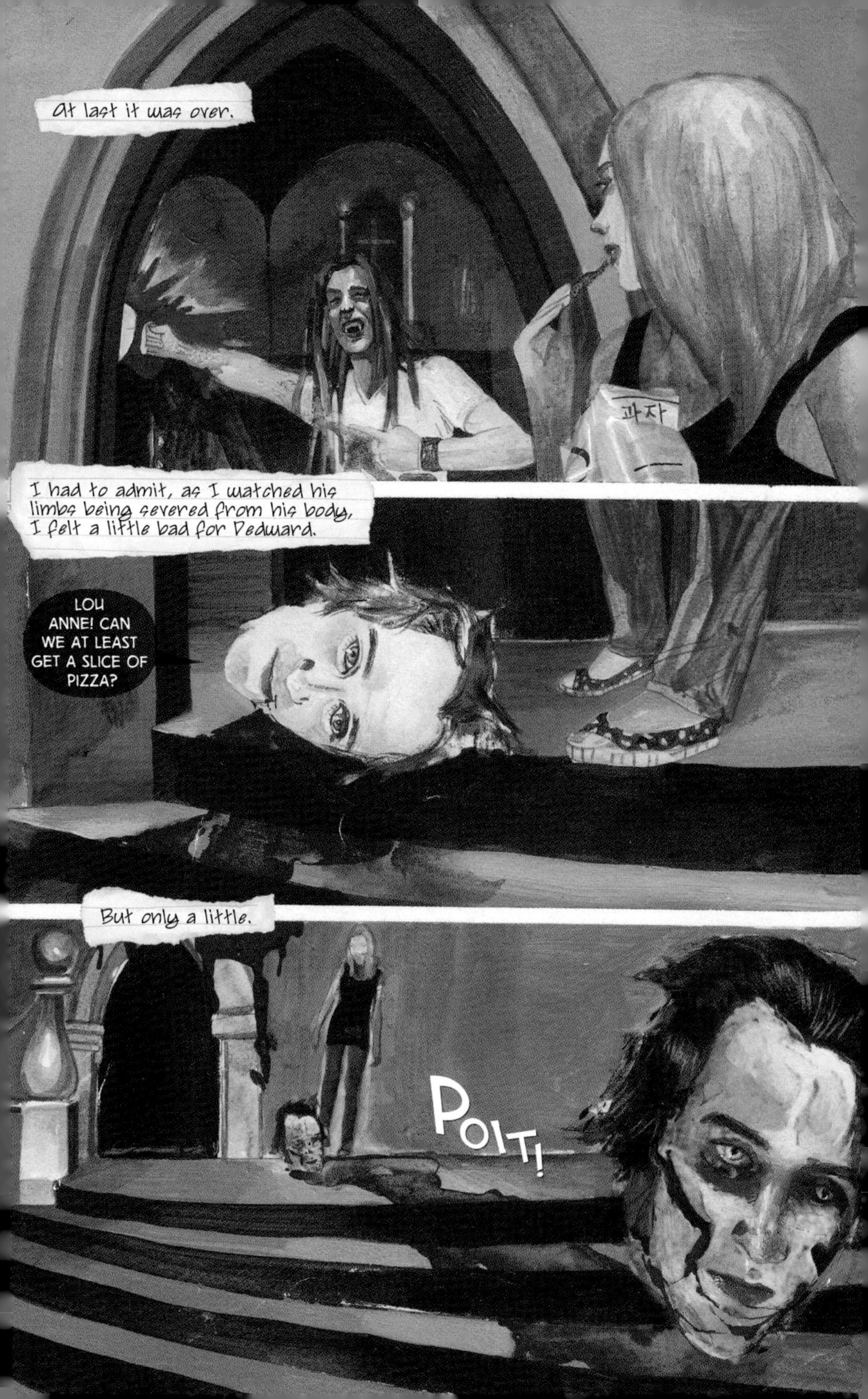
at last it was over.
과자
I had to admit, as I watched his limbs being severed from his body, I felt a little bad for Dedward.
LOU ANNE! CAN WE AT LEAST GET A SLICE OF PIZZA?
But only a little.
POIT!

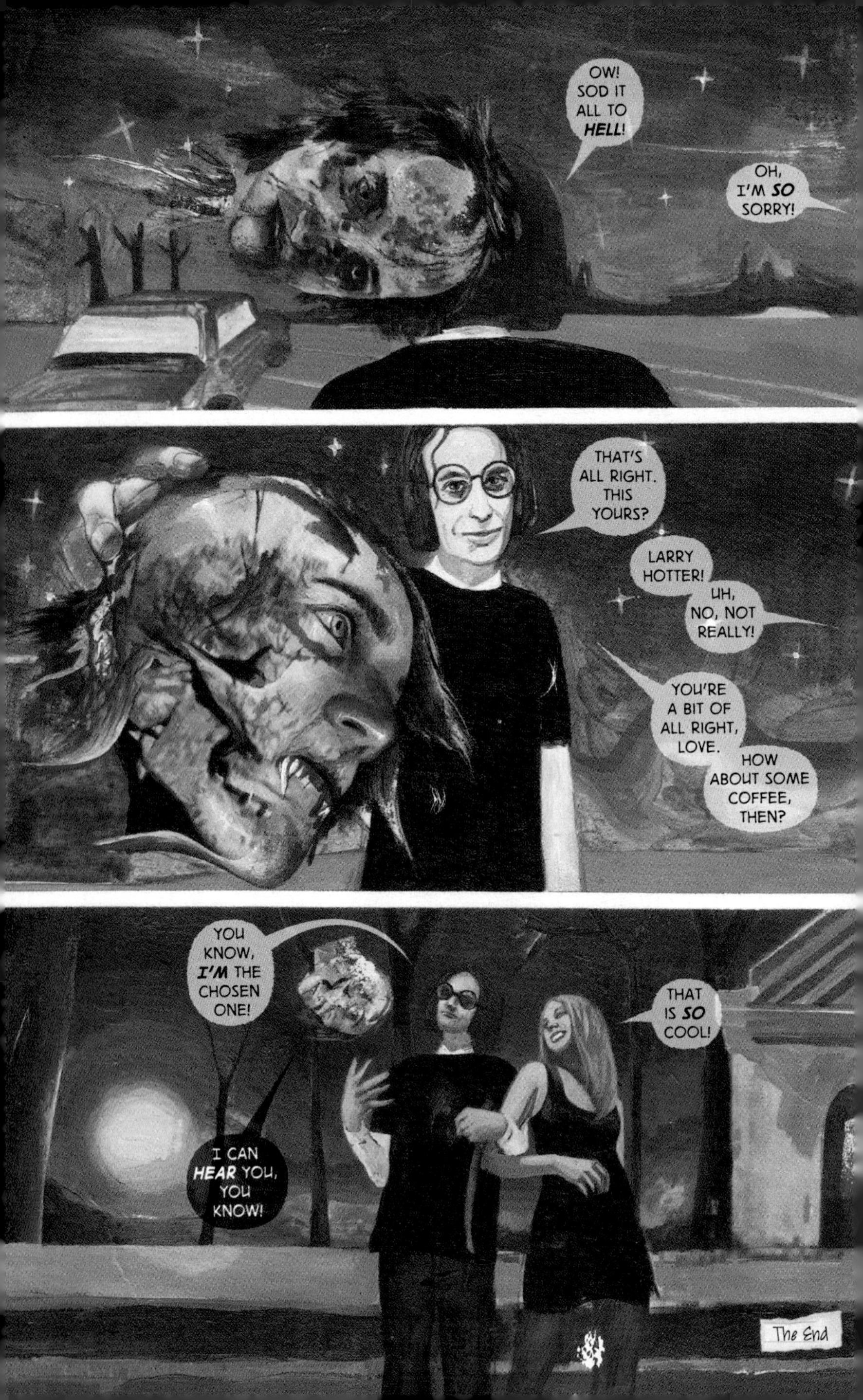
OW! SOD IT ALL TO HELL!
OH, I'M SO SORRY!
THAT'S ALL RIGHT. THIS YOURS?
LARRY HOTTER!
UH, NO, NOT REALLY!
YOU'RE A BIT OF ALL RIGHT, LOVE.
HOW ABOUT SOME COFFEE, THEN?
YOU KNOW, I'M THE CHOSEN ONE!
THAT IS SO COOL!
I CAN HEAR YOU, YOU KNOW!
The End

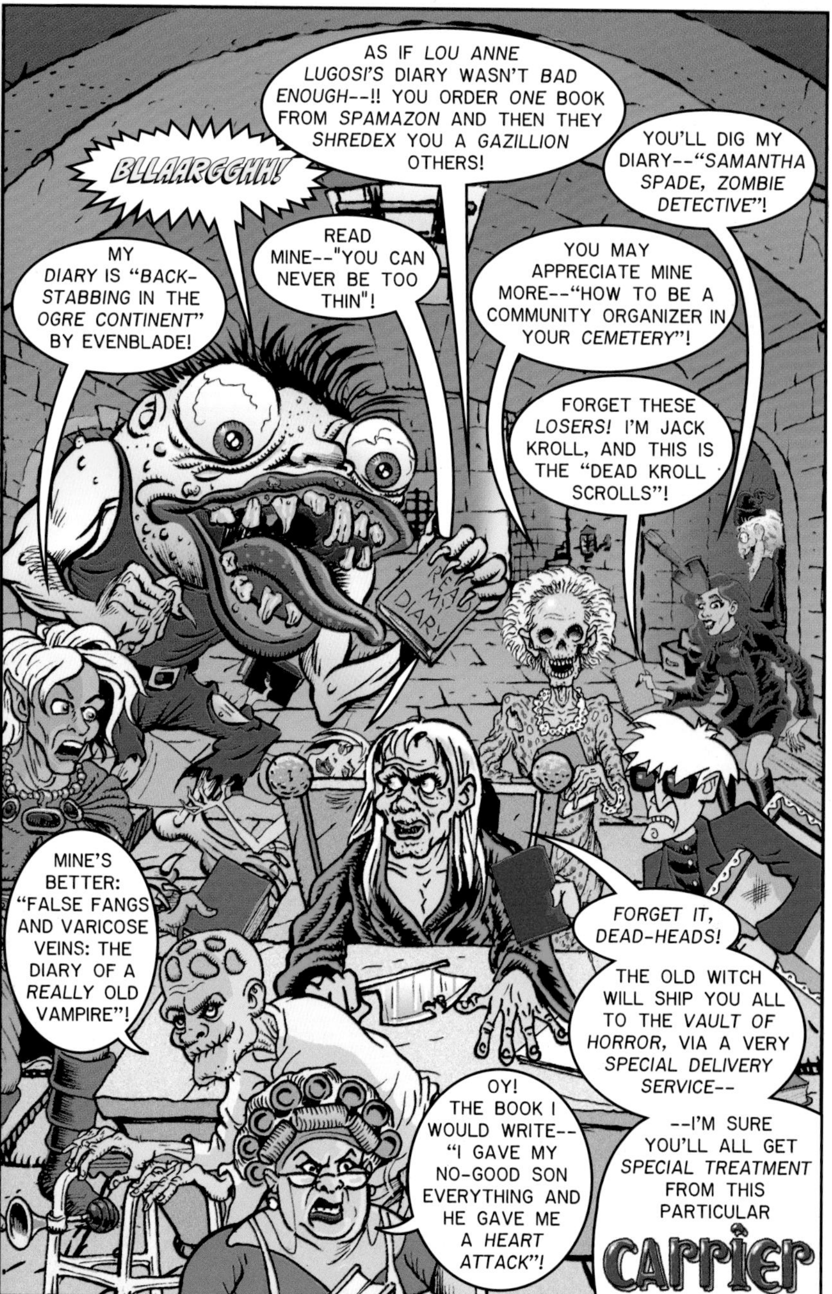
BLLAARGGHH!
AS IF LOU ANNE LUGOSI'S DIARY WASN'T BAD ENOUGH--!! YOU ORDER ONE BOOK FROM SPAMAZON AND THEN THEY SHREDEX YOU A GAZILLION OTHERS!
YOU'LL DIG MY DIARY--"SAMANTHA SPADE, ZOMBIE DETECTIVE"!
MY DIARY IS "BACK-STABBING IN THE OGRE CONTINENT" BY EVENBLADE!
READ MINE--"YOU CAN NEVER BE TOO THIN"!
YOU MAY APPRECIATE MINE MORE--"HOW TO BE A COMMUNITY ORGANIZER IN YOUR CEMETERY"!
FORGET THESE LOSERS! I'M JACK KROLL, AND THIS IS THE "DEAD KROLL SCROLLS"!
READ MY DIARY
MINE'S BETTER: "FALSE FANGS AND VARICOSE VEINS: THE DIARY OF A REALLY OLD VAMPIRE"!
FORGET IT, DEAD-HEADS!
THE OLD WITCH WILL SHIP YOU ALL TO THE VAULT OF HORROR, VIA A VERY SPECIAL DELIVERY SERVICE--
OY! THE BOOK I WOULD WRITE--"I GAVE MY NO-GOOD SON EVERYTHING AND HE GAVE ME A HEART ATTACK"!
--I'M SURE YOU'LL ALL GET SPECIAL TREATMENT FROM THIS PARTICULAR
CARRIER

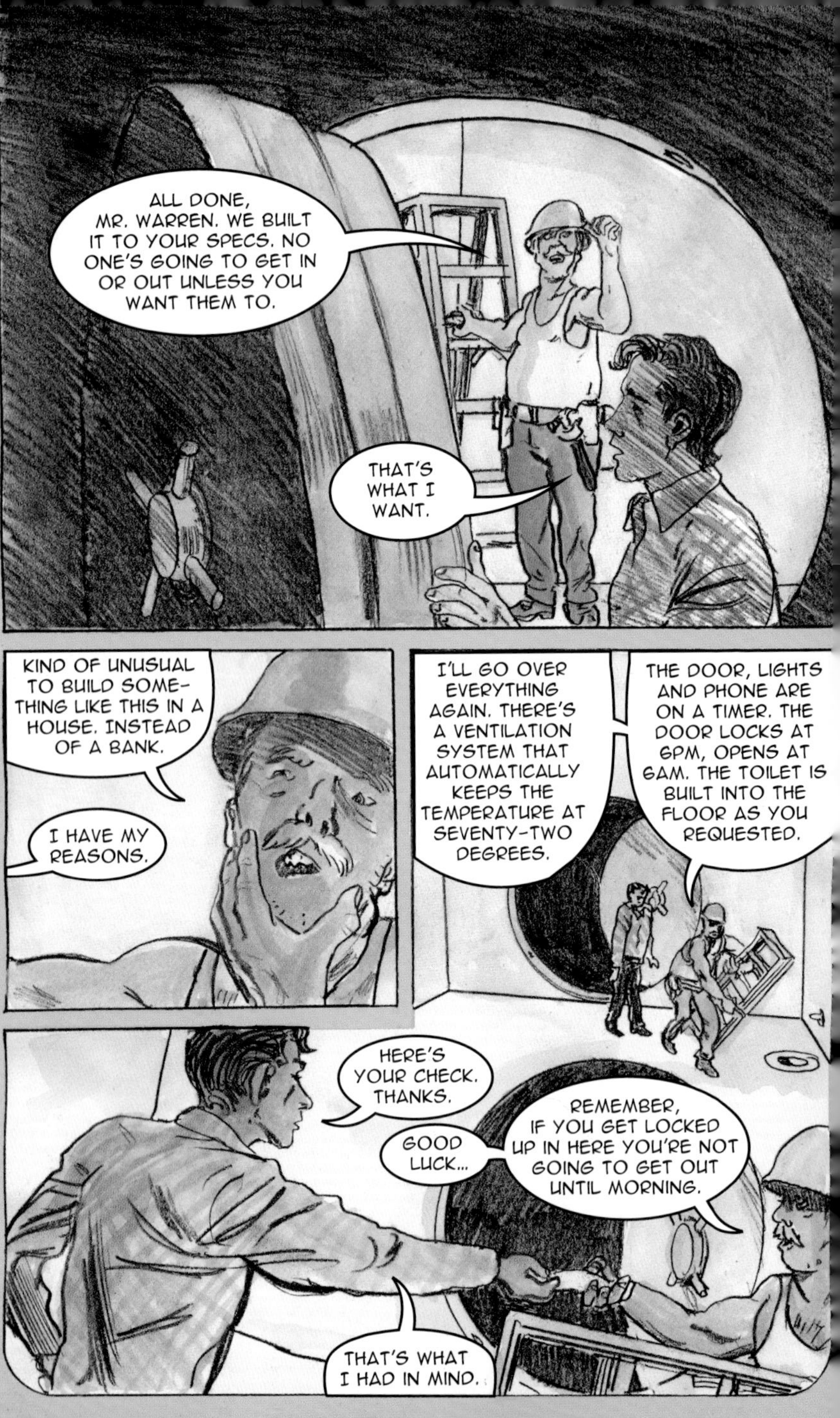
ALL DONE, MR. WARREN. WE BUILT IT TO YOUR SPECS. NO ONE'S GOING TO GET IN OR OUT UNLESS YOU WANT THEM TO.
THAT'S WHAT I WANT.
KIND OF UNUSUAL TO BUILD SOME-THING LIKE THIS IN A HOUSE. INSTEAD OF A BANK.
I HAVE MY REASONS.
I'LL GO OVER EVERYTHING AGAIN. THERE'S A VENTILATION SYSTEM THAT AUTOMATICALLY KEEPS THE TEMPERATURE AT SEVENTY-TWO DEGREES.
THE DOOR, LIGHTS AND PHONE ARE ON A TIMER. THE DOOR LOCKS AT 6PM, OPENS AT 6AM. THE TOILET IS BUILT INTO THE FLOOR AS YOU REQUESTED.
HERE'S YOUR CHECK. THANKS.
REMEMBER, IF YOU GET LOCKED UP IN HERE YOU'RE NOT GOING TO GET OUT UNTIL MORNING.
GOOD LUCK...
THAT'S WHAT I HAD IN MIND.

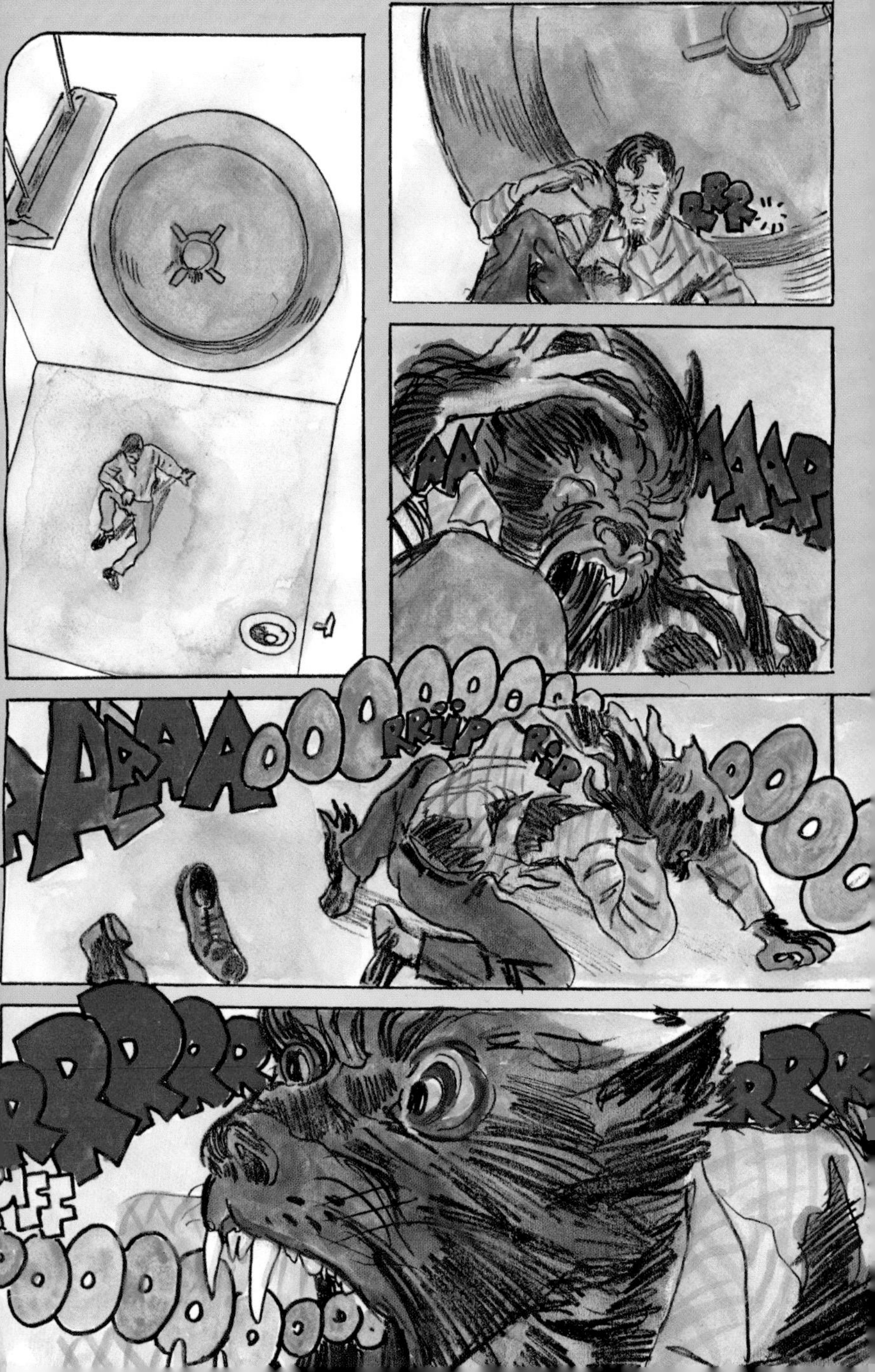

RRR
AA
AAAAR
AAAAAAOOOOOOO
RRIIP
RIP
OOOOO
RRRRR
RRR
OOOOOOW

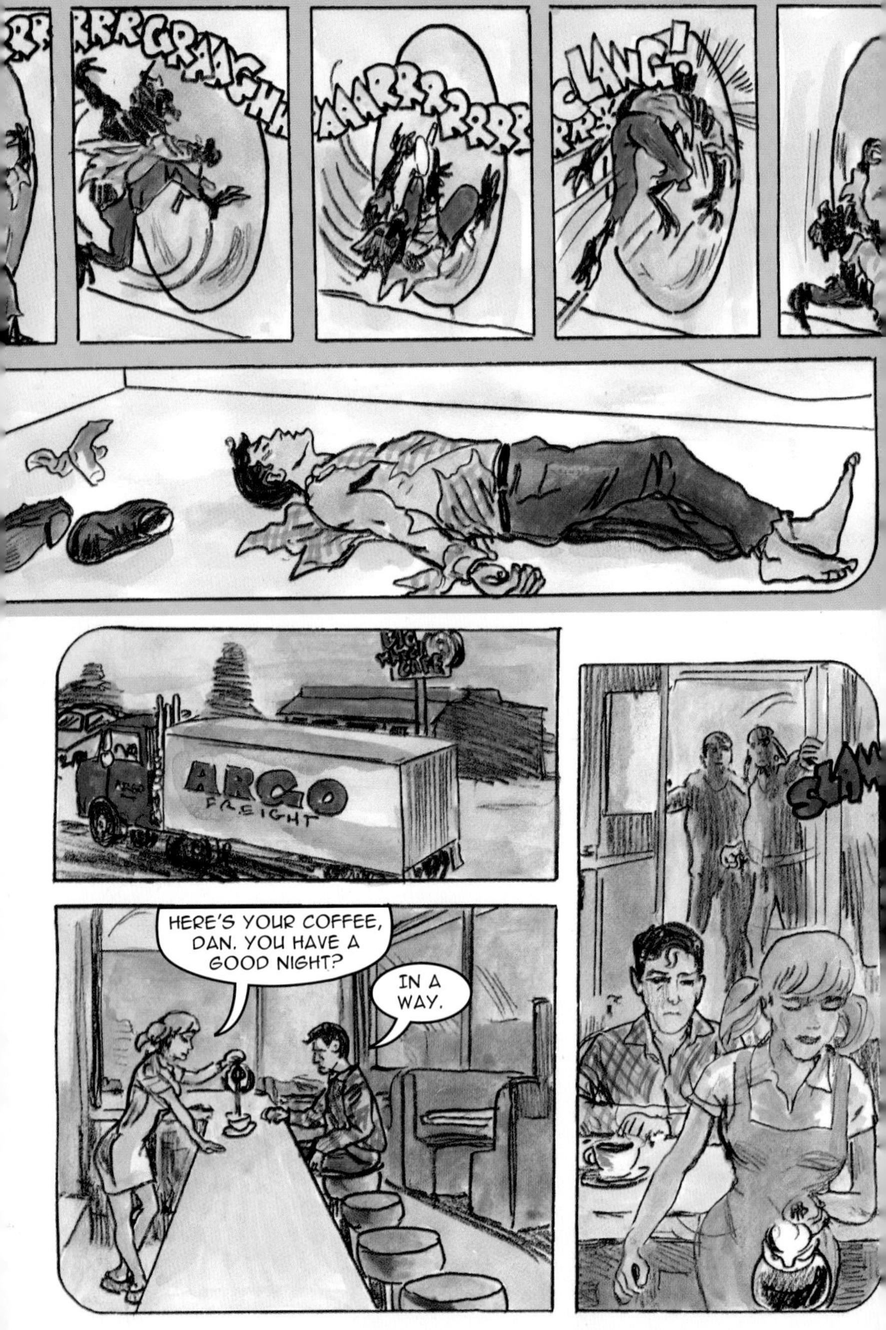
CLANG!
ARGO
FREIGHT
HERE'S YOUR COFFEE, DAN. YOU HAVE A GOOD NIGHT?
IN A WAY.

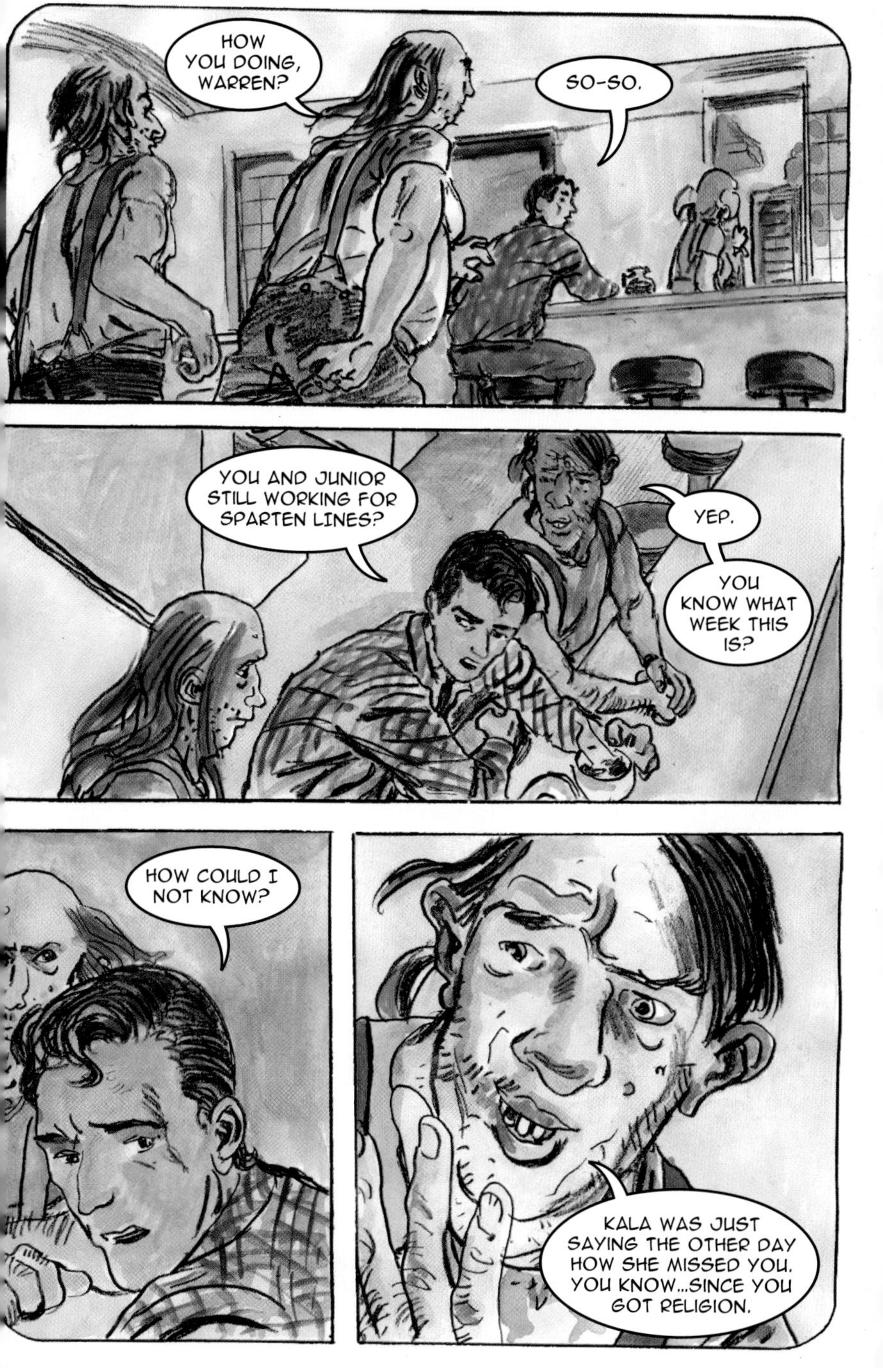
HOW YOU DOING, WARREN?
SO-SO.
YOU AND JUNIOR STILL WORKING FOR SPARTEN LINES?
YEP.
YOU KNOW WHAT WEEK THIS IS?
HOW COULD I NOT KNOW?
KALA WAS JUST SAYING THE OTHER DAY HOW SHE MISSED YOU. YOU KNOW...SINCE YOU GOT RELIGION.

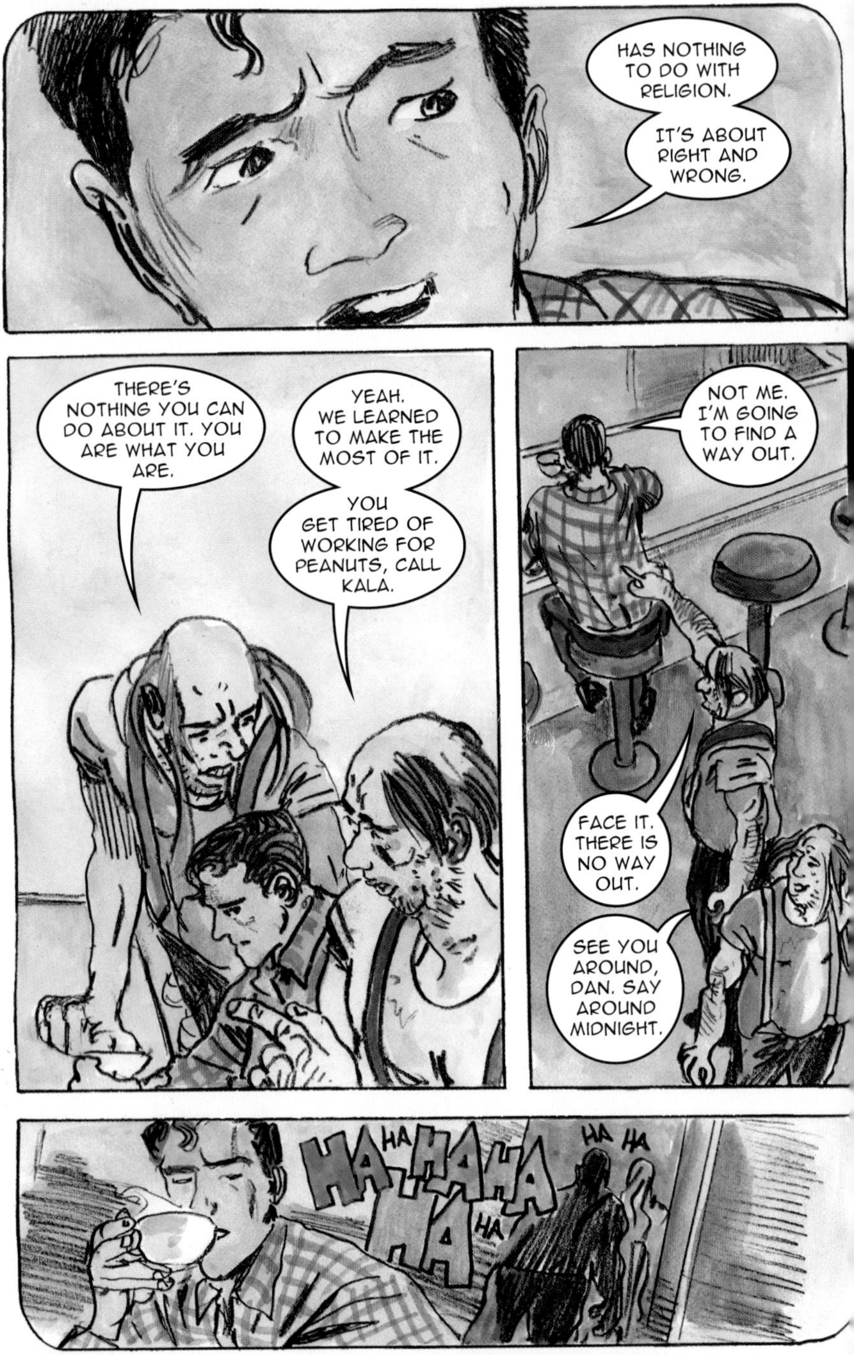
HAS NOTHING TO DO WITH RELIGION.
IT'S ABOUT RIGHT AND WRONG.
THERE'S NOTHING YOU CAN DO ABOUT IT. YOU ARE WHAT YOU ARE.
YEAH. WE LEARNED TO MAKE THE MOST OF IT.
YOU GET TIRED OF WORKING FOR PEANUTS, CALL KALA.
NOT ME. I'M GOING TO FIND A WAY OUT.
FACE IT. THERE IS NO WAY OUT.
SEE YOU AROUND, DAN. SAY AROUND MIDNIGHT.
HA HA HAHA HA HA
HA HA

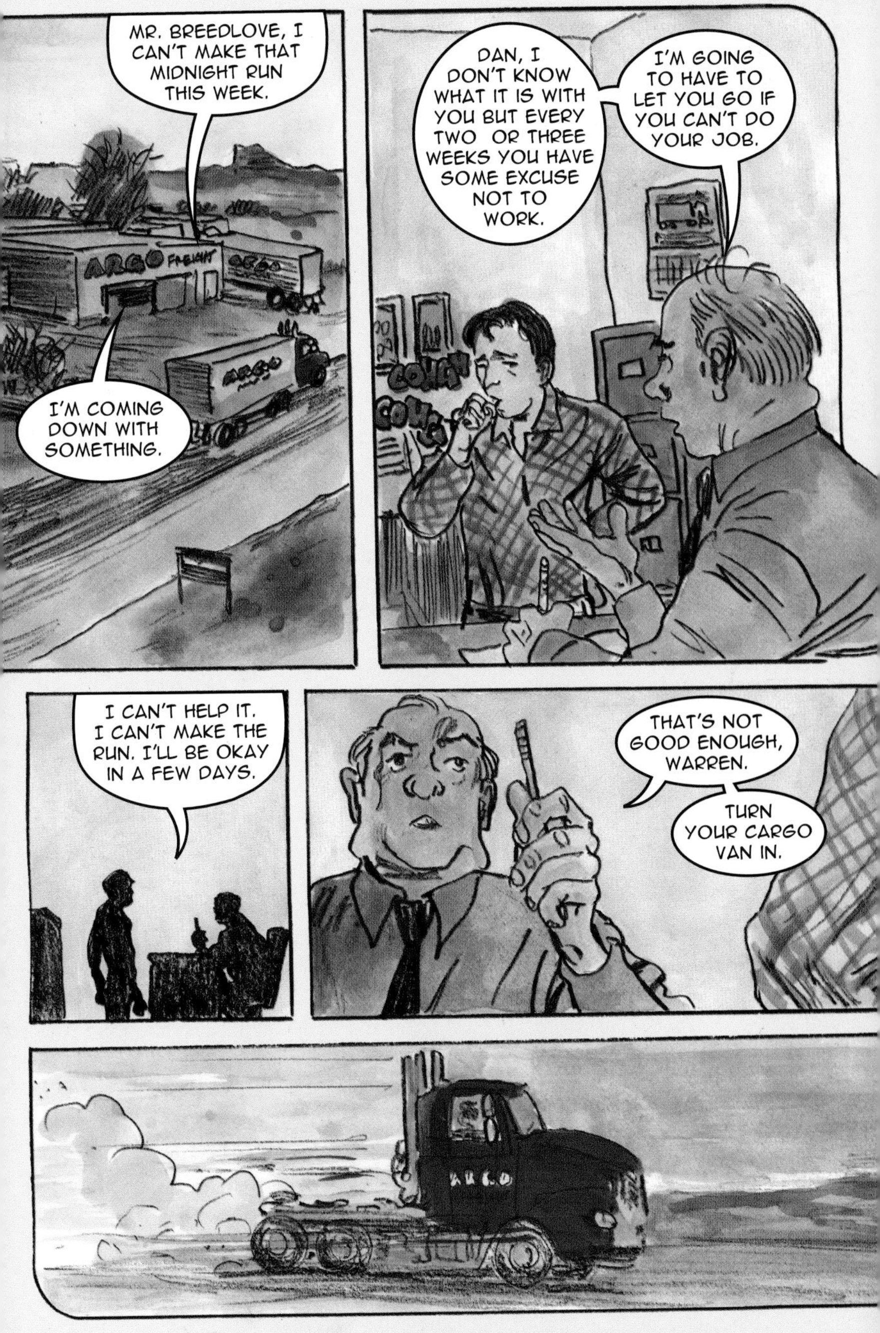
MR. BREEDLOVE, I CAN'T MAKE THAT MIDNIGHT RUN THIS WEEK.
I'M COMING DOWN WITH SOMETHING.
DAN, I DON'T KNOW WHAT IT IS WITH YOU BUT EVERY TWO OR THREE WEEKS YOU HAVE SOME EXCUSE NOT TO WORK.
I'M GOING TO HAVE TO LET YOU GO IF YOU CAN'T DO YOUR JOB.
I CAN'T HELP IT. I CAN'T MAKE THE RUN. I'LL BE OKAY IN A FEW DAYS.
THAT'S NOT GOOD ENOUGH, WARREN.
TURN YOUR CARGO VAN IN.

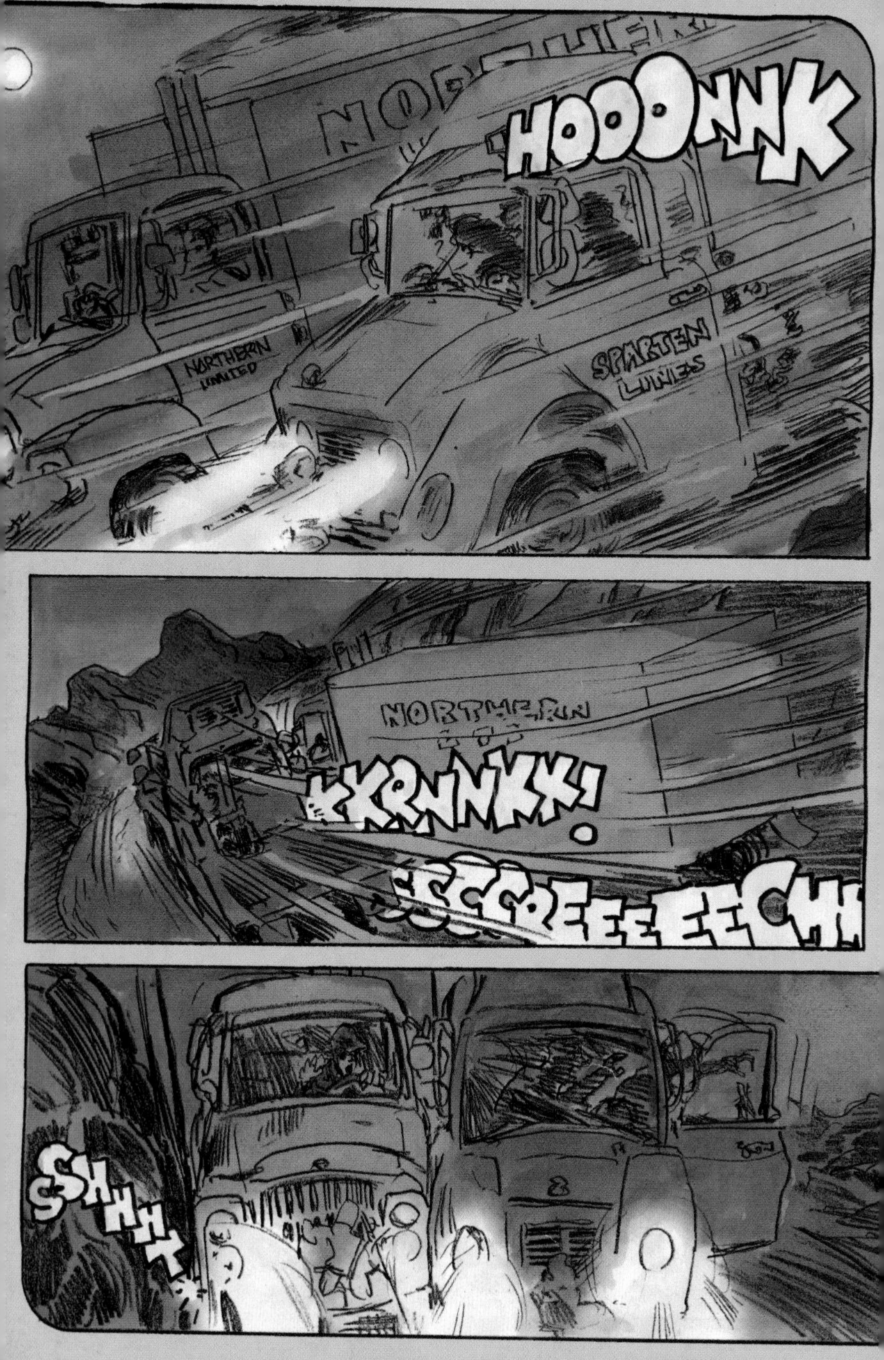
NORTHERN
HOOONNK
NORTHERN UNITED
SPARTEN LINES
NORTHERN
KRNNKK!
SCCREEEEECH
SSHHHK

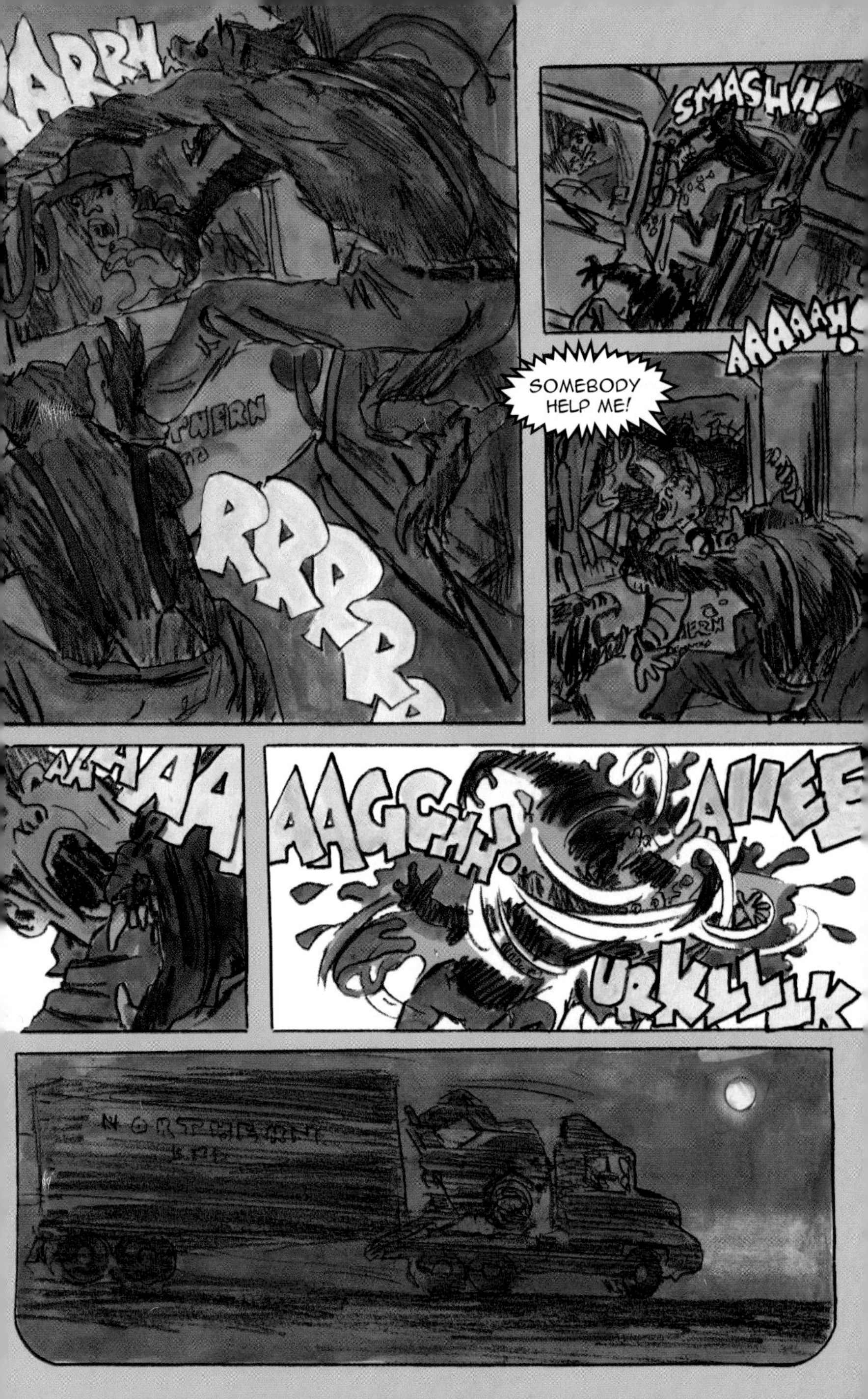
ARRH
RRRR
SMASHH!
AAAAH!
SOMEBODY HELP ME!
AAAAAA
AAGGHH!
AIIEE
URKLLLK

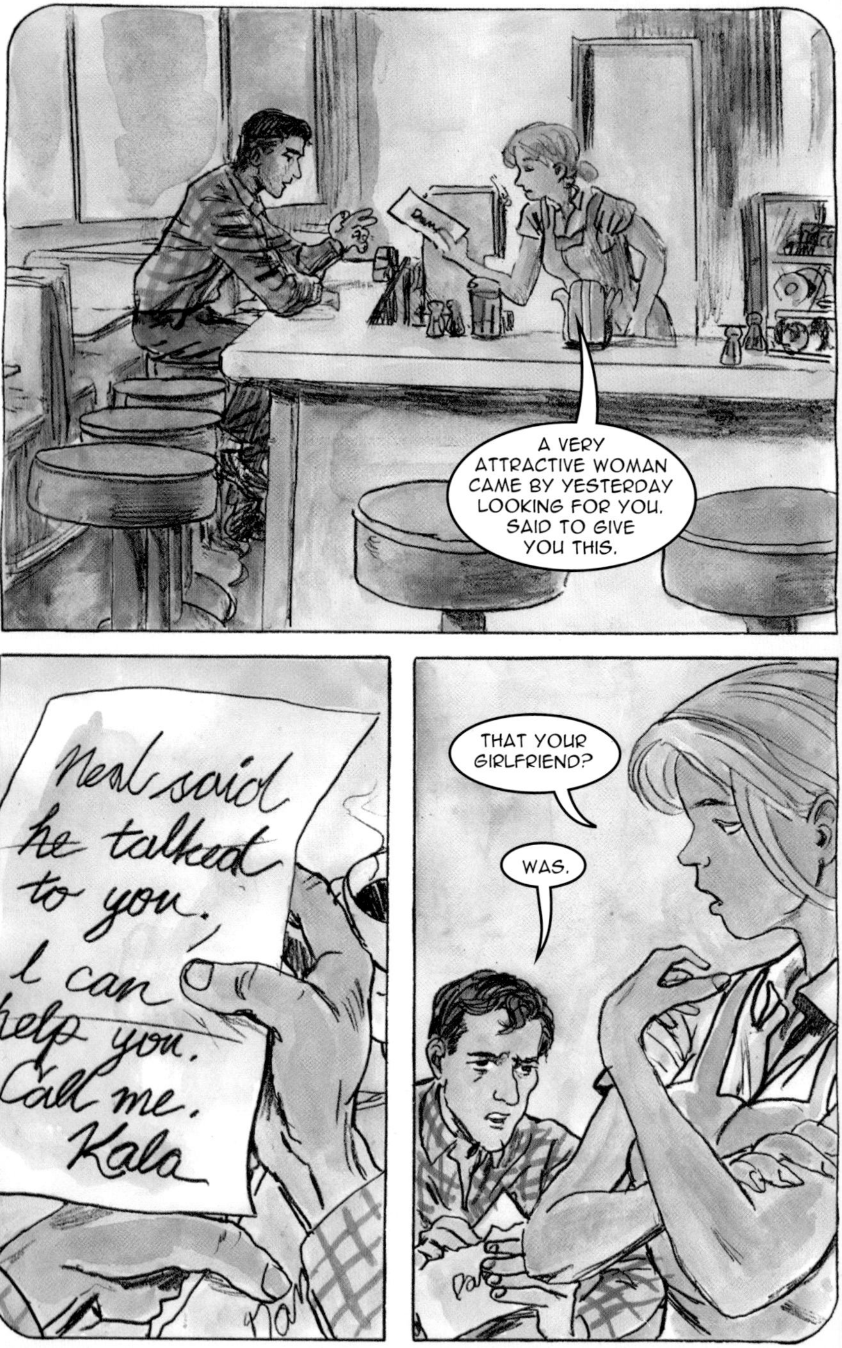
A VERY ATTRACTIVE WOMAN CAME BY YESTERDAY LOOKING FOR YOU. SAID TO GIVE YOU THIS.
Neal said he talked to you. I can help you. Call me. Kala
THAT YOUR GIRLFRIEND?
WAS.

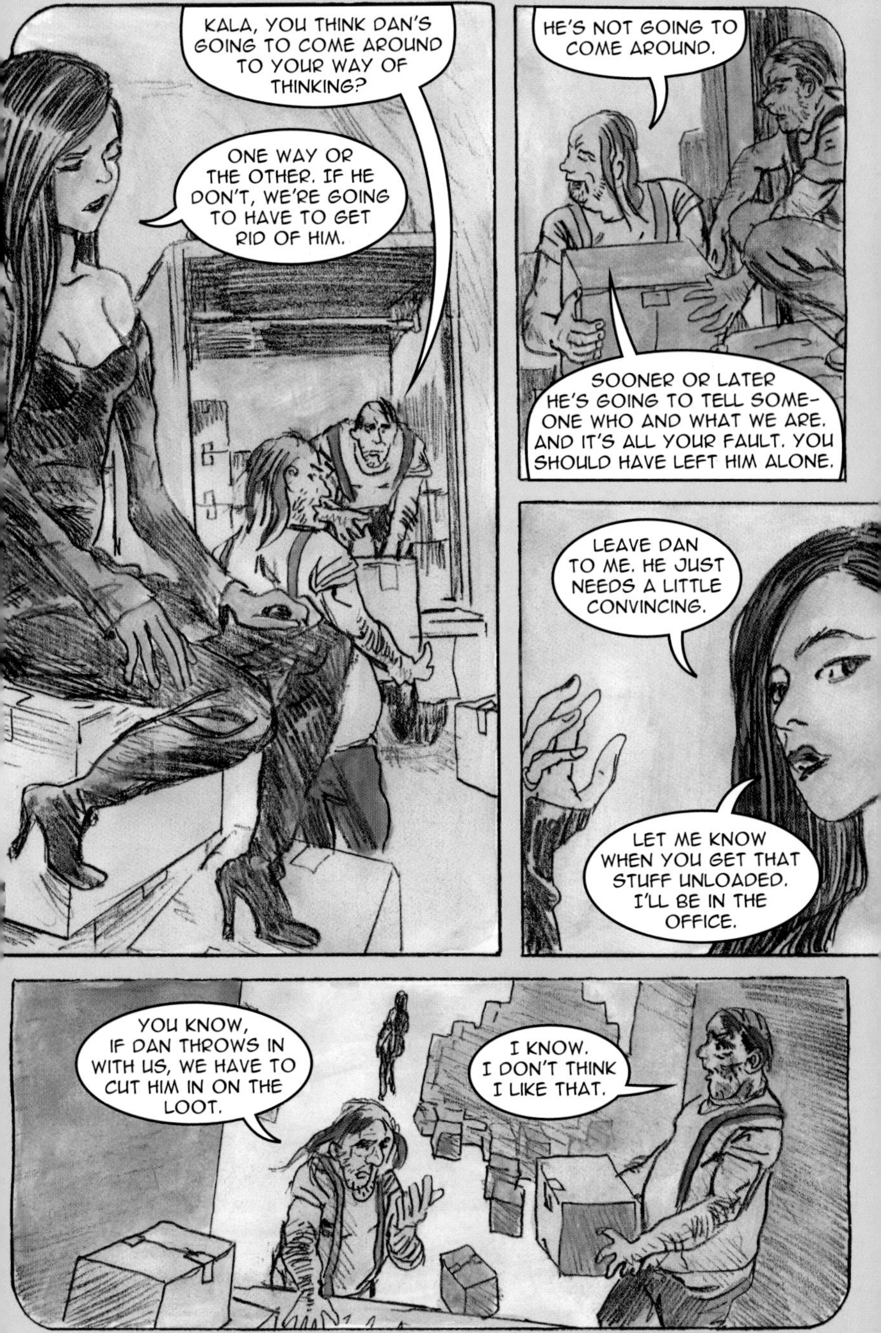
KALA, YOU THINK DAN'S GOING TO COME AROUND TO YOUR WAY OF THINKING?
ONE WAY OR THE OTHER. IF HE DON'T, WE'RE GOING TO HAVE TO GET RID OF HIM.
HE'S NOT GOING TO COME AROUND.
SOONER OR LATER HE'S GOING TO TELL SOME-ONE WHO AND WHAT WE ARE. AND IT'S ALL YOUR FAULT. YOU SHOULD HAVE LEFT HIM ALONE.
LEAVE DAN TO ME. HE JUST NEEDS A LITTLE CONVINCING.
LET ME KNOW WHEN YOU GET THAT STUFF UNLOADED. I'LL BE IN THE OFFICE.
YOU KNOW, IF DAN THROWS IN WITH US, WE HAVE TO CUT HIM IN ON THE LOOT.
I KNOW. I DON'T THINK I LIKE THAT.

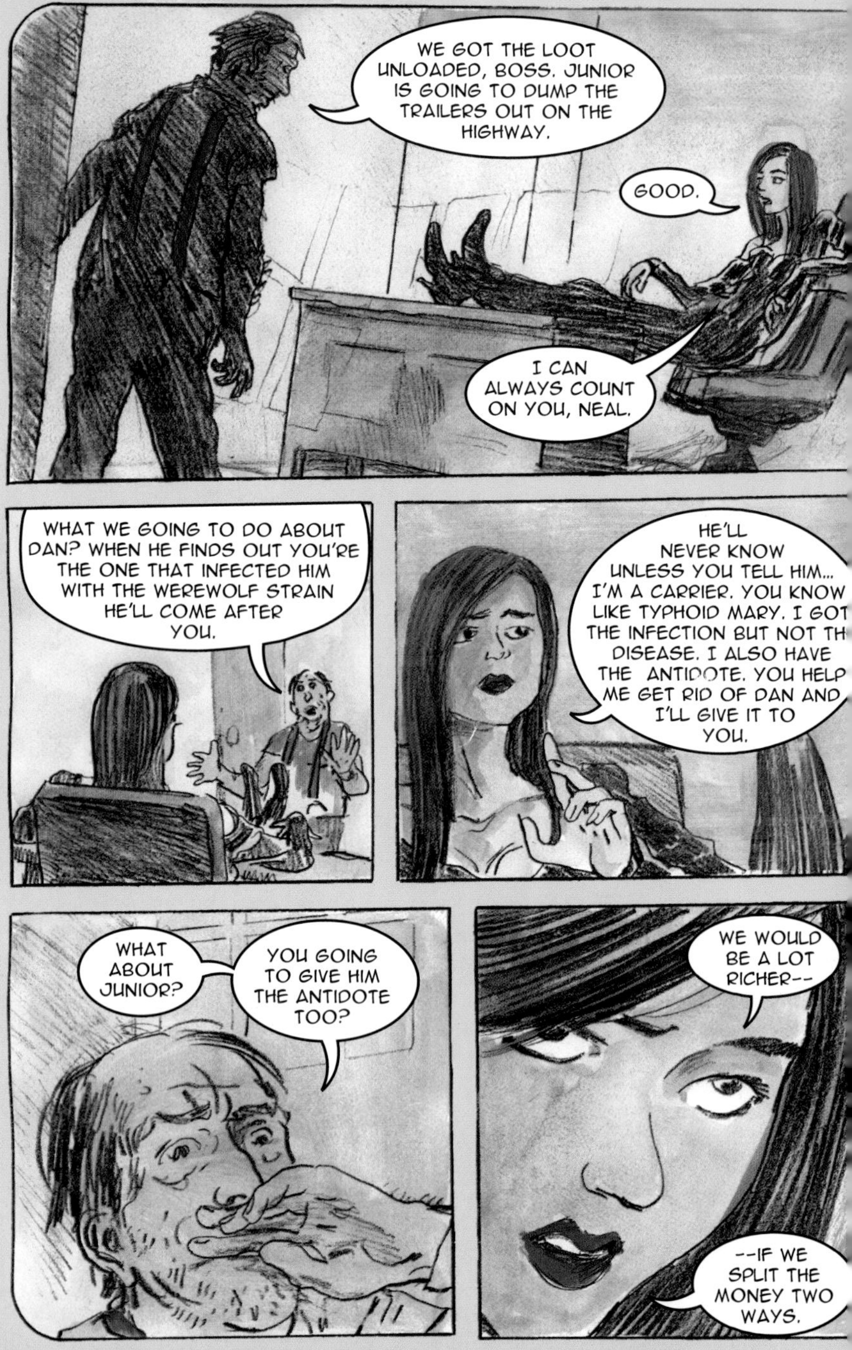
WE GOT THE LOOT UNLOADED, BOSS. JUNIOR IS GOING TO DUMP THE TRAILERS OUT ON THE HIGHWAY.
GOOD.
I CAN ALWAYS COUNT ON YOU, NEAL.
WHAT WE GOING TO DO ABOUT DAN? WHEN HE FINDS OUT YOU'RE THE ONE THAT INFECTED HIM WITH THE WEREWOLF STRAIN HE'LL COME AFTER YOU.
HE'LL NEVER KNOW UNLESS YOU TELL HIM... I'M A CARRIER. YOU KNOW LIKE TYPHOID MARY. I GOT THE INFECTION BUT NOT TH DISEASE. I ALSO HAVE THE ANTIDOTE. YOU HELP ME GET RID OF DAN AND I'LL GIVE IT TO YOU.
WHAT ABOUT JUNIOR?
YOU GOING TO GIVE HIM THE ANTIDOTE TOO?
WE WOULD BE A LOT RICHER--
--IF WE SPLIT THE MONEY TWO WAYS.

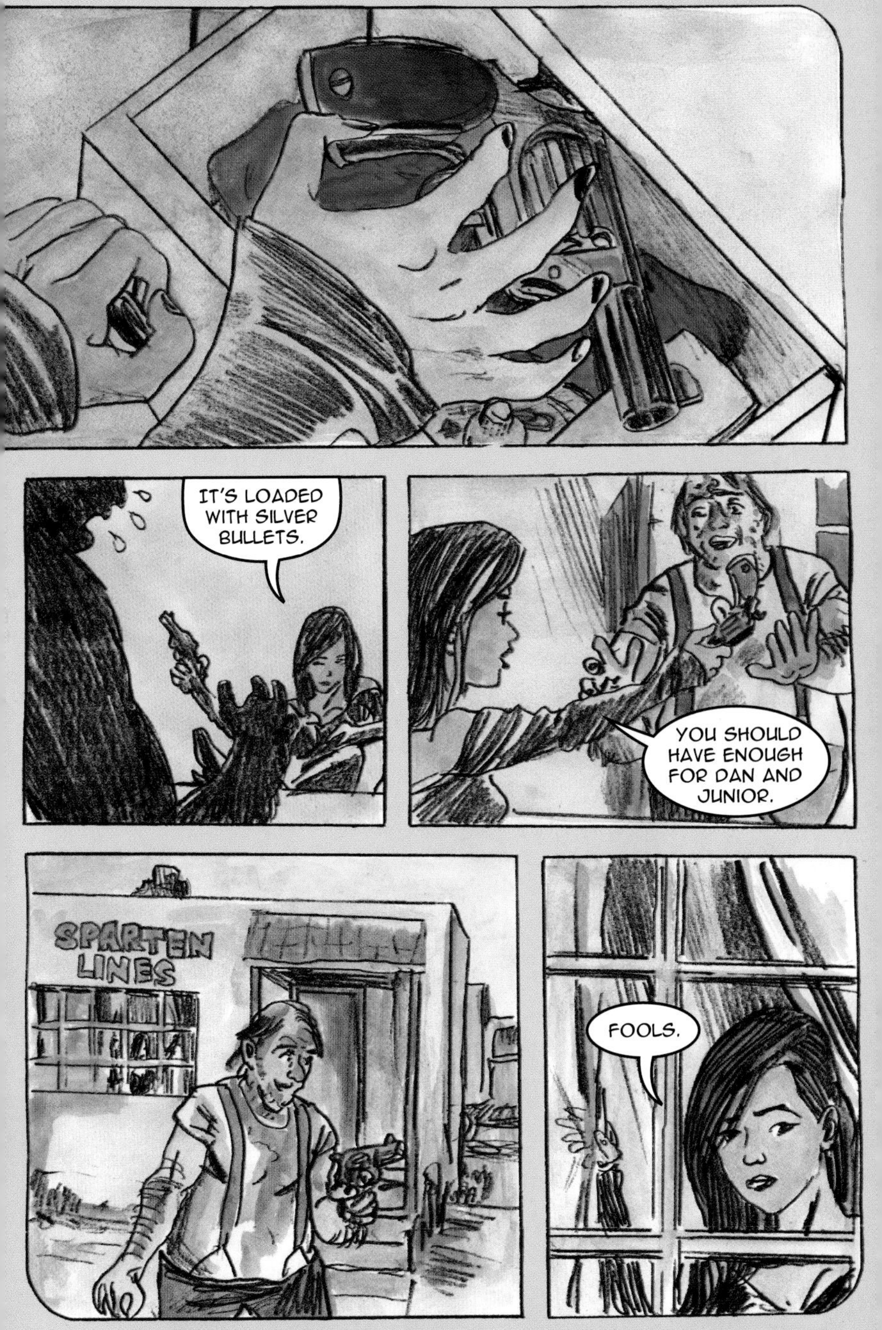
IT'S LOADED WITH SILVER BULLETS.
YOU SHOULD HAVE ENOUGH FOR DAN AND JUNIOR.
SPARTEN LINES
FOOLS.

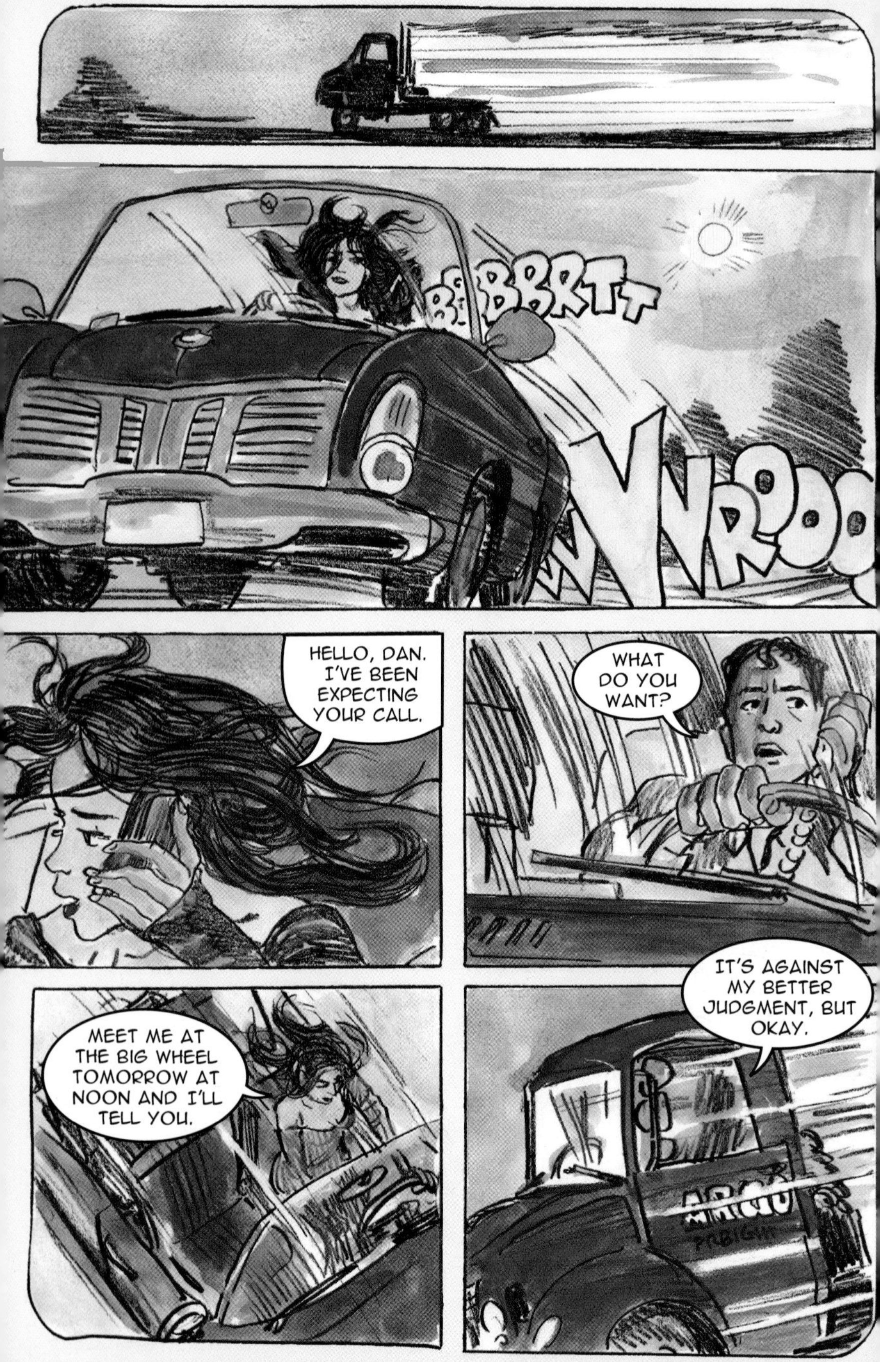
HELLO, DAN. I'VE BEEN EXPECTING YOUR CALL.
WHAT DO YOU WANT?
MEET ME AT THE BIG WHEEL TOMORROW AT NOON AND I'LL TELL YOU.
IT'S AGAINST MY BETTER JUDGMENT, BUT OKAY.

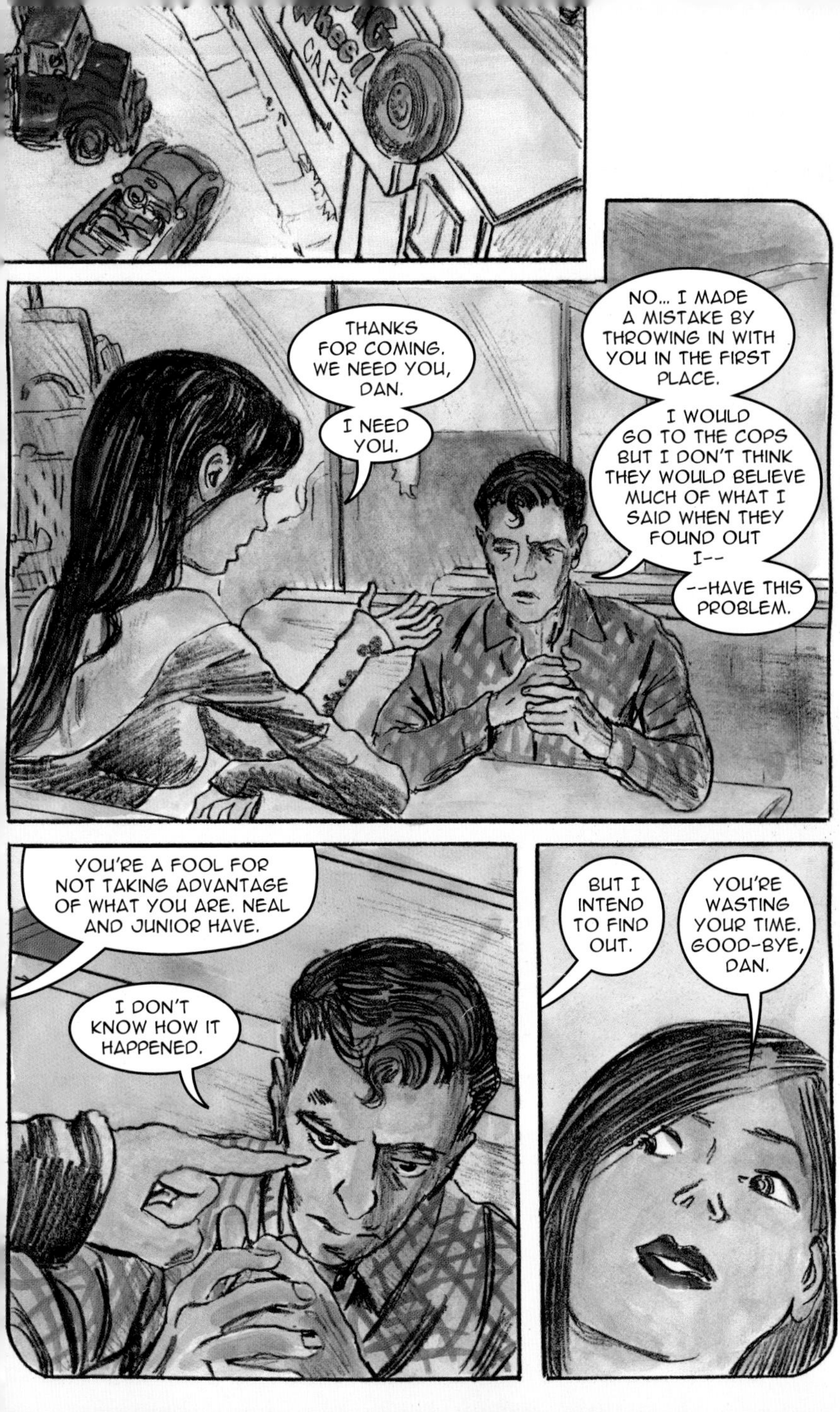
THANKS FOR COMING. WE NEED YOU, DAN.
I NEED YOU.
NO... I MADE A MISTAKE BY THROWING IN WITH YOU IN THE FIRST PLACE.
I WOULD GO TO THE COPS BUT I DON'T THINK THEY WOULD BELIEVE MUCH OF WHAT I SAID WHEN THEY FOUND OUT I--
--HAVE THIS PROBLEM.
YOU'RE A FOOL FOR NOT TAKING ADVANTAGE OF WHAT YOU ARE. NEAL AND JUNIOR HAVE.
I DON'T KNOW HOW IT HAPPENED.
BUT I INTEND TO FIND OUT.
YOU'RE WASTING YOUR TIME. GOOD-BYE, DAN.

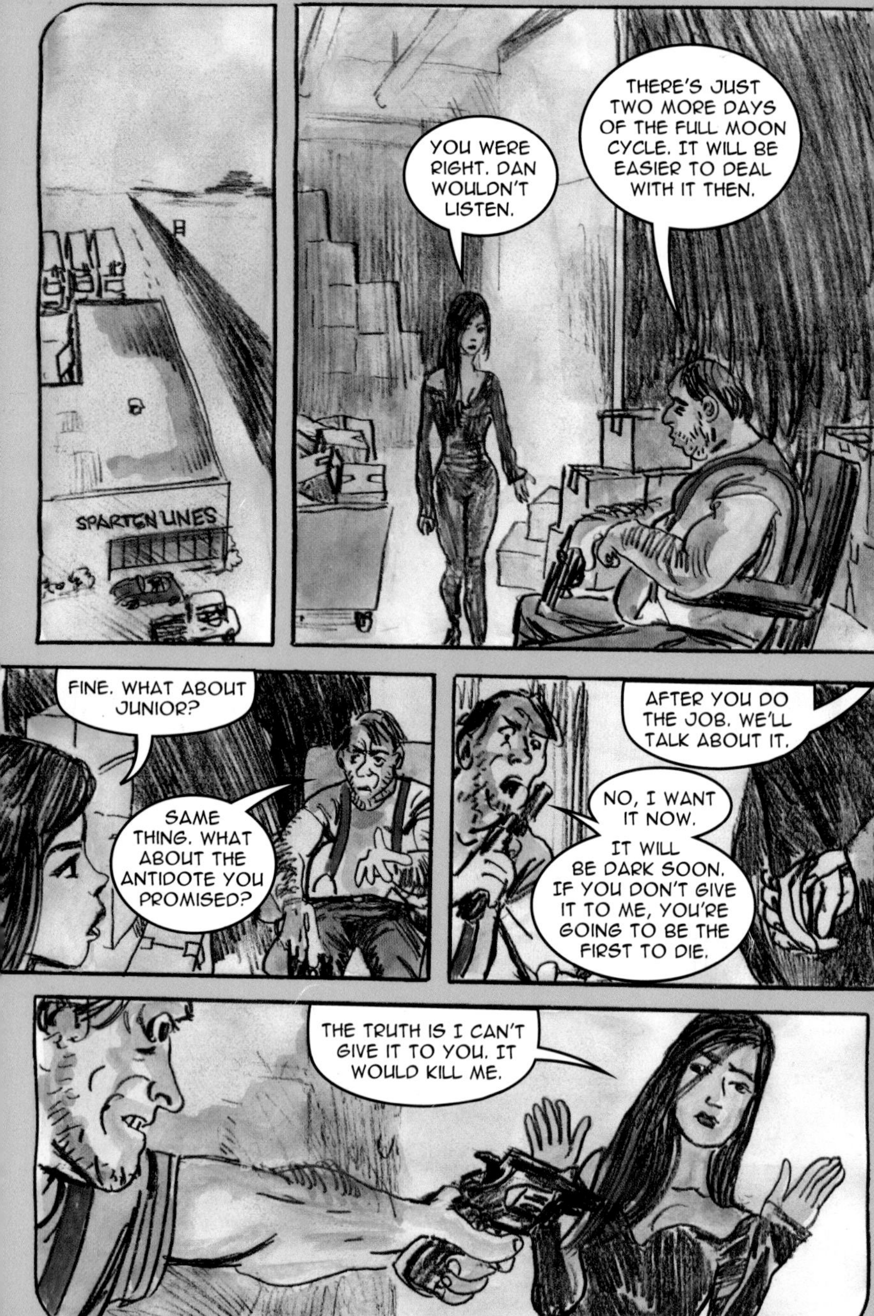
SPARTEN LINES
YOU WERE RIGHT. DAN WOULDN'T LISTEN.
THERE'S JUST TWO MORE DAYS OF THE FULL MOON CYCLE. IT WILL BE EASIER TO DEAL WITH IT THEN.
FINE. WHAT ABOUT JUNIOR?
SAME THING. WHAT ABOUT THE ANTIDOTE YOU PROMISED?
AFTER YOU DO THE JOB. WE'LL TALK ABOUT IT.
NO, I WANT IT NOW.
IT WILL BE DARK SOON. IF YOU DON'T GIVE IT TO ME, YOU'RE GOING TO BE THE FIRST TO DIE.
THE TRUTH IS I CAN'T GIVE IT TO YOU. IT WOULD KILL ME.

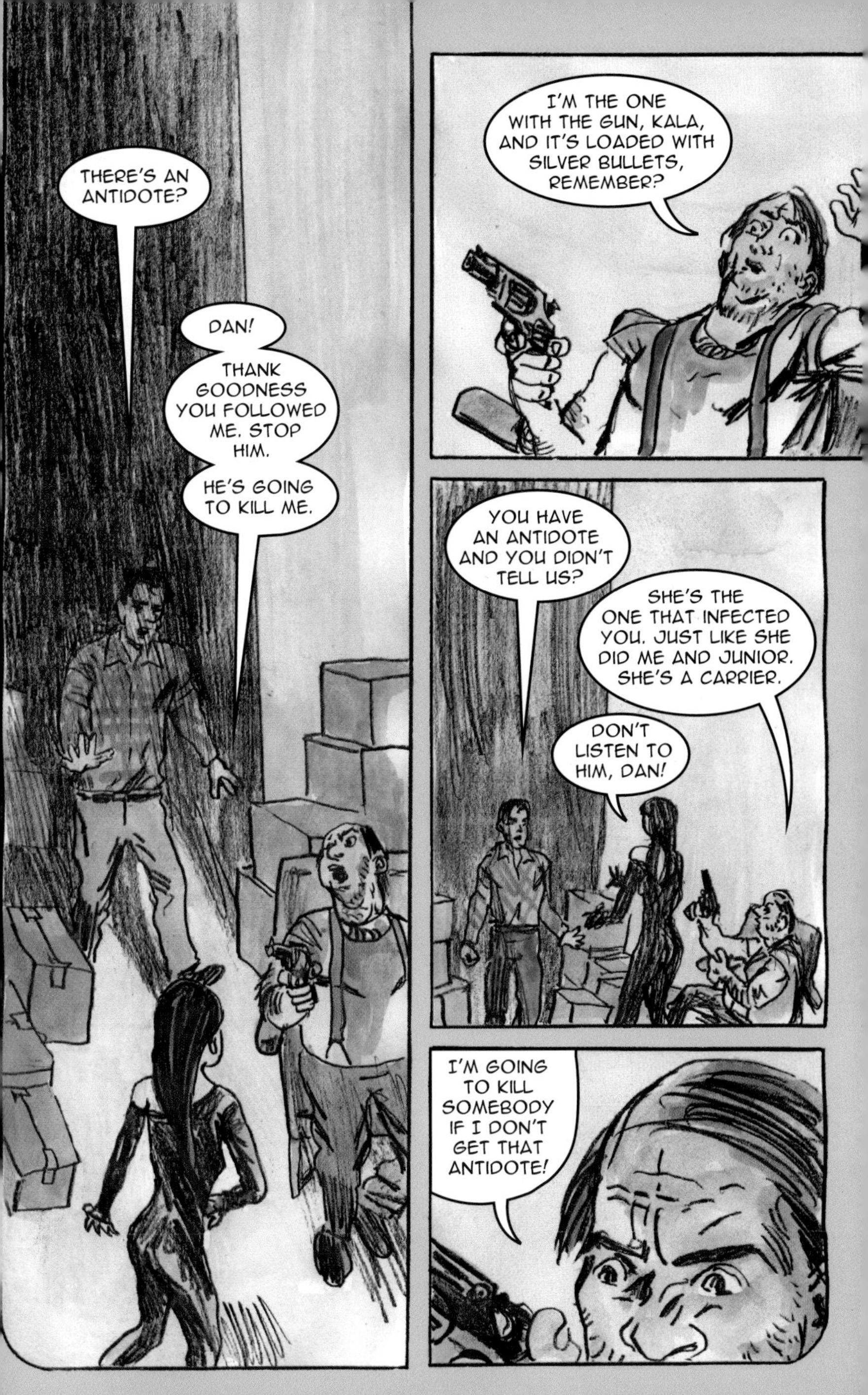
THERE'S AN ANTIDOTE?
DAN!
THANK GOODNESS YOU FOLLOWED ME. STOP HIM.
HE'S GOING TO KILL ME.
I'M THE ONE WITH THE GUN, KALA, AND IT'S LOADED WITH SILVER BULLETS, REMEMBER?
YOU HAVE AN ANTIDOTE AND YOU DIDN'T TELL US?
SHE'S THE ONE THAT INFECTED YOU. JUST LIKE SHE DID ME AND JUNIOR. SHE'S A CARRIER.
DON'T LISTEN TO HIM, DAN!
I'M GOING TO KILL SOMEBODY IF I DON'T GET THAT ANTIDOTE!

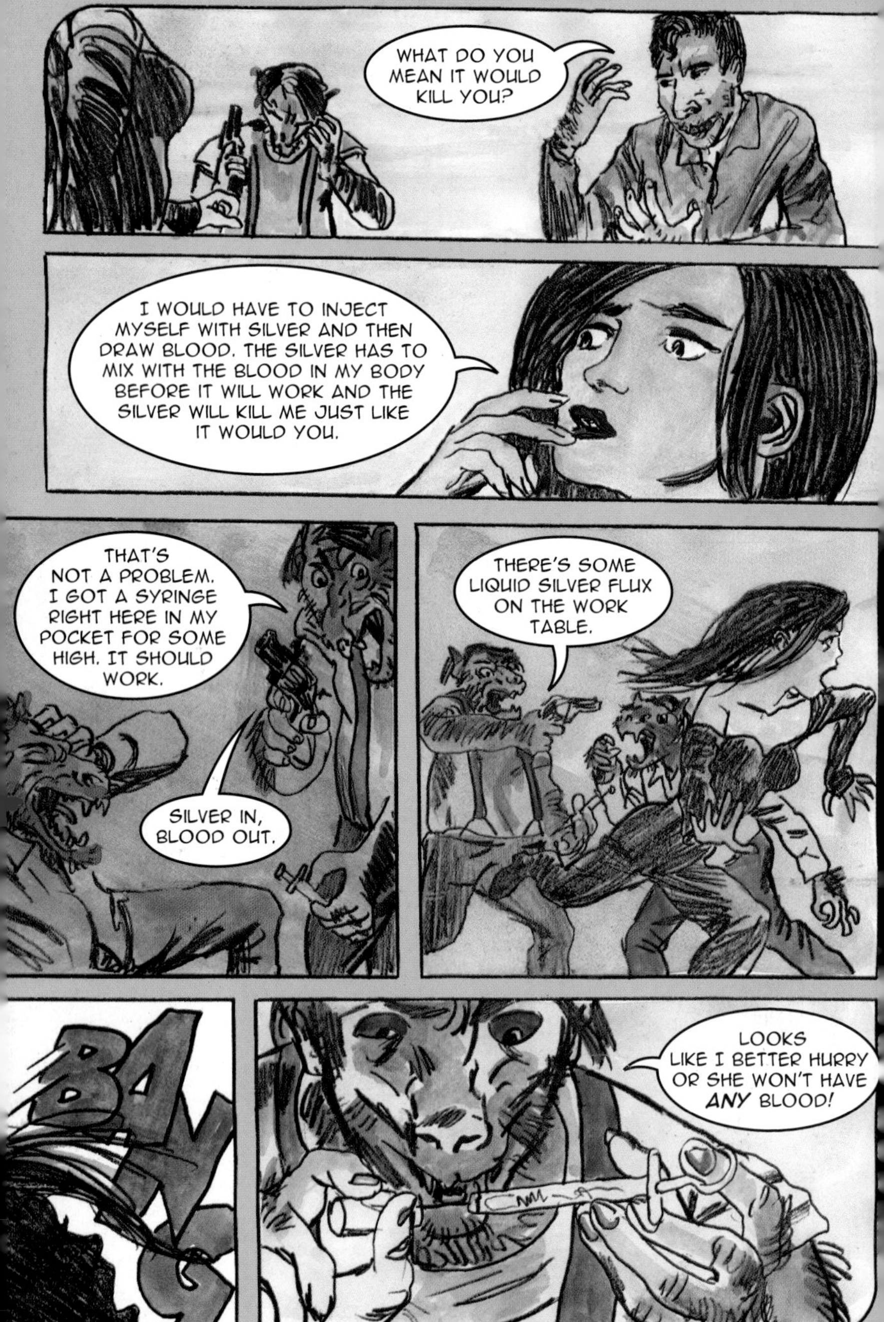
WHAT DO YOU MEAN IT WOULD KILL YOU?
I WOULD HAVE TO INJECT MYSELF WITH SILVER AND THEN DRAW BLOOD. THE SILVER HAS TO MIX WITH THE BLOOD IN MY BODY BEFORE IT WILL WORK AND THE SILVER WILL KILL ME JUST LIKE IT WOULD YOU.
THAT'S NOT A PROBLEM. I GOT A SYRINGE RIGHT HERE IN MY POCKET FOR SOME HIGH. IT SHOULD WORK.
SILVER IN, BLOOD OUT.
THERE'S SOME LIQUID SILVER FLUX ON THE WORK TABLE.
BAM
LOOKS LIKE I BETTER HURRY OR SHE WON'T HAVE *ANY* BLOOD!

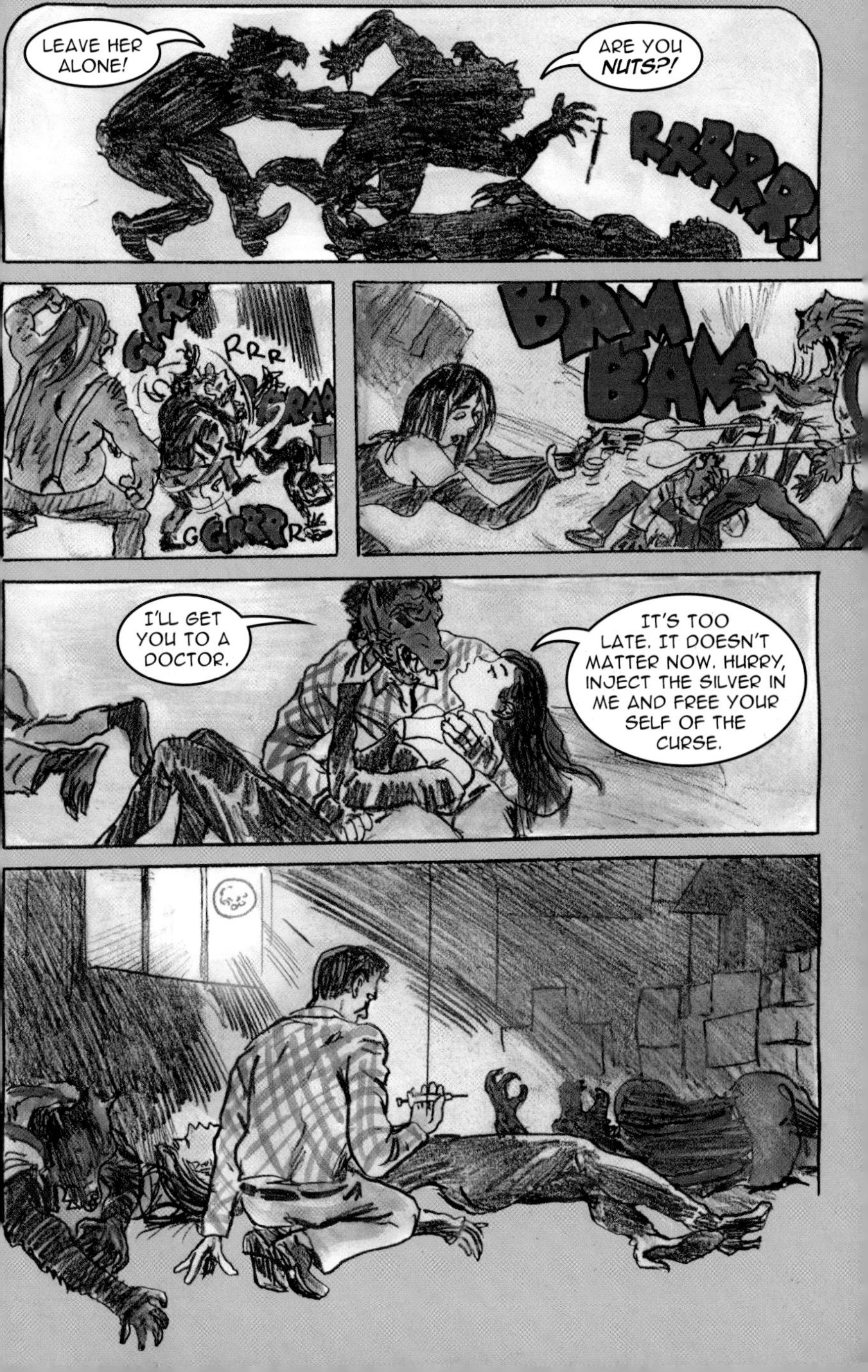
LEAVE HER ALONE!
ARE YOU NUTS?!
RRRRR!
RRR
BAM BAM!
I'LL GET YOU TO A DOCTOR.
IT'S TOO LATE. IT DOESN'T MATTER NOW. HURRY, INJECT THE SILVER IN ME AND FREE YOUR SELF OF THE CURSE.

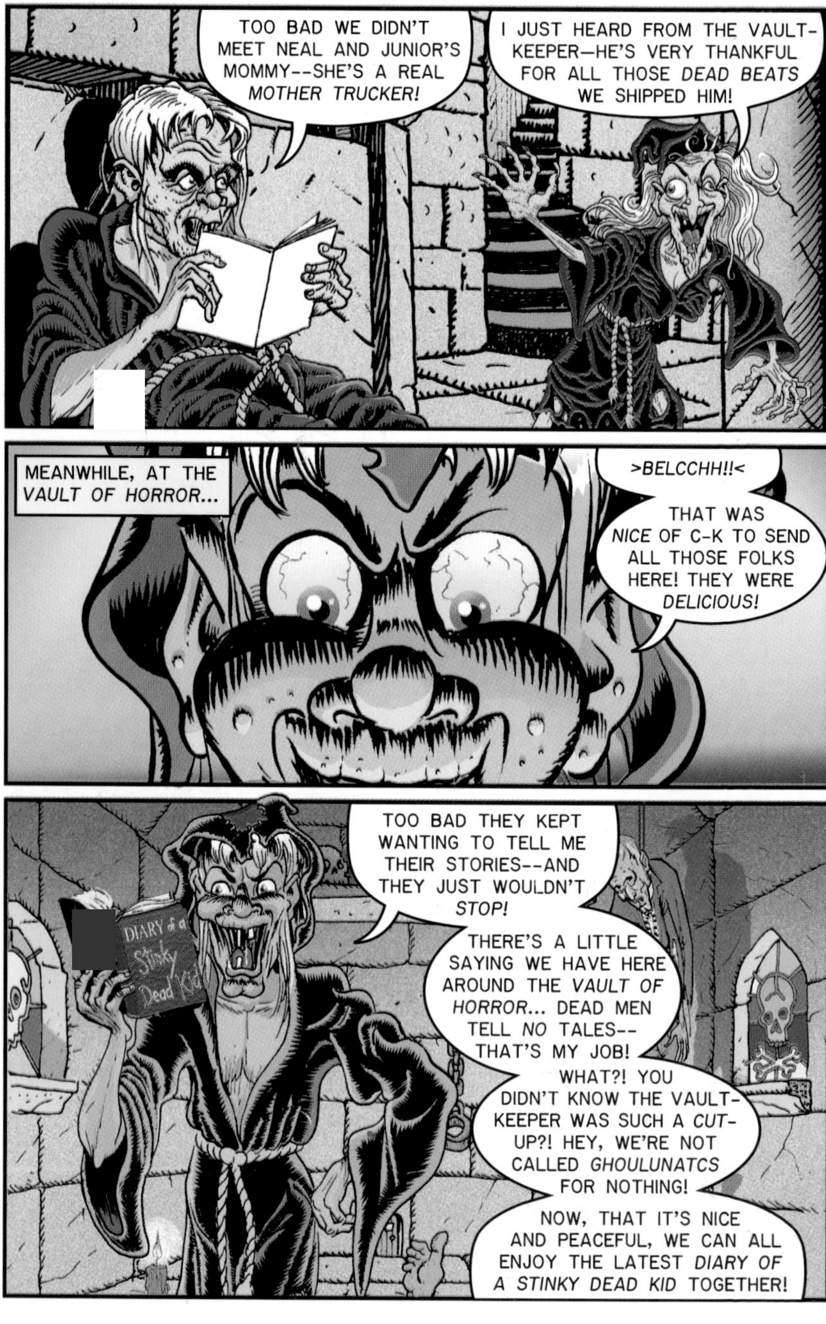
TOO BAD WE DIDN'T MEET NEAL AND JUNIOR'S MOMMY--SHE'S A REAL *MOTHER TRUCKER!*
I JUST HEARD FROM THE VAULT-KEEPER—HE'S VERY THANKFUL FOR ALL THOSE *DEAD BEATS* WE SHIPPED HIM!
MEANWHILE, AT THE *VAULT OF HORROR...*
>BELCCHH!!<
THAT WAS *NICE* OF C-K TO SEND ALL THOSE FOLKS HERE! THEY WERE *DELICIOUS!*
TOO BAD THEY KEPT WANTING TO TELL ME THEIR STORIES--AND THEY JUST WOULDN'T *STOP!*
DIARY of a Stinky Dead Kid
THERE'S A LITTLE SAYING WE HAVE HERE AROUND THE *VAULT OF HORROR*... DEAD MEN TELL *NO* TALES--THAT'S MY JOB!
WHAT?! YOU DIDN'T KNOW THE VAULT-KEEPER WAS SUCH A *CUT-UP*?! HEY, WE'RE NOT CALLED *GHOULUNATCS* FOR NOTHING!
NOW, THAT IT'S NICE AND PEACEFUL, WE CAN ALL ENJOY THE LATEST *DIARY OF A STINKY DEAD KID* TOGETHER!

NOVEMBER

TUESDAY

So here I am stuck in the cemetery just because the neighbors complained about the "strange" smell. I tried showering, but pieces of me kept coming off.

Mom says it's just until she can find the right spell to return me to the living, but if I had any breath, I wouldn't be holding it.

I was worried it'd be creepy here, but it turns out there's a pretty decent bunch of Z's hanging around, nicer than some of the kids at school, anyway. You never know who's dead until you take the time to find out.

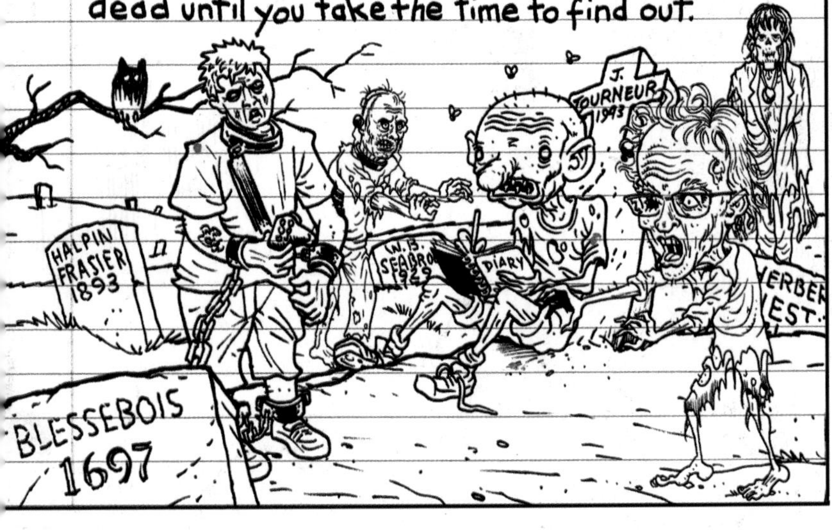

J. TOURNEUR 1943
HALPIN FRASIER 1893
W.B. SEABROOK 1929
DIARY
ERBER EST.
BLESSEBOIS 1697

In one night, I met Ed, Garth, Bub and Boyle! I wasn't sure what kind of Z Boyle was. I didn't want to say anything, but frankly he seemed more sick than dead.

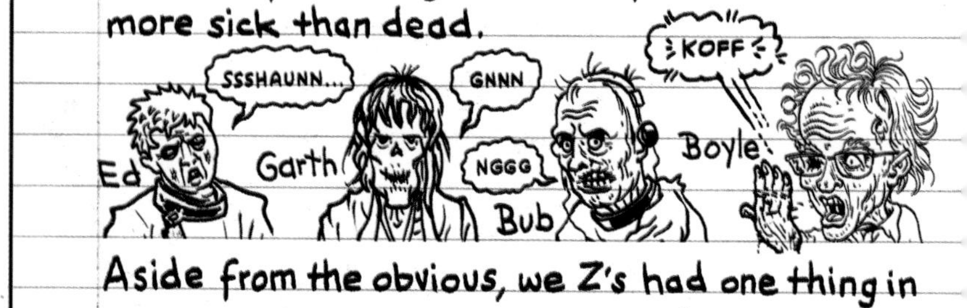
SSSHAUNN...
Ed
Garth
GNNN
NGGG
Bub
KOFF
Boyle

Aside from the obvious, we Z's had one thing in common. We were bored silly. About the most exciting thing that happened was when Crowley came by to visit.

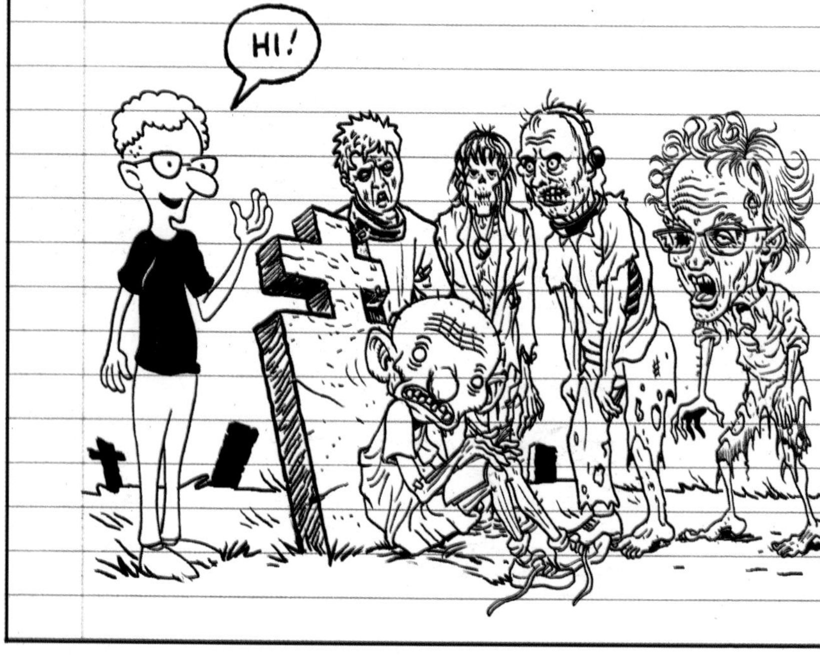
HI!

And the most exciting thing about that was trying to stop everyone from eating him.

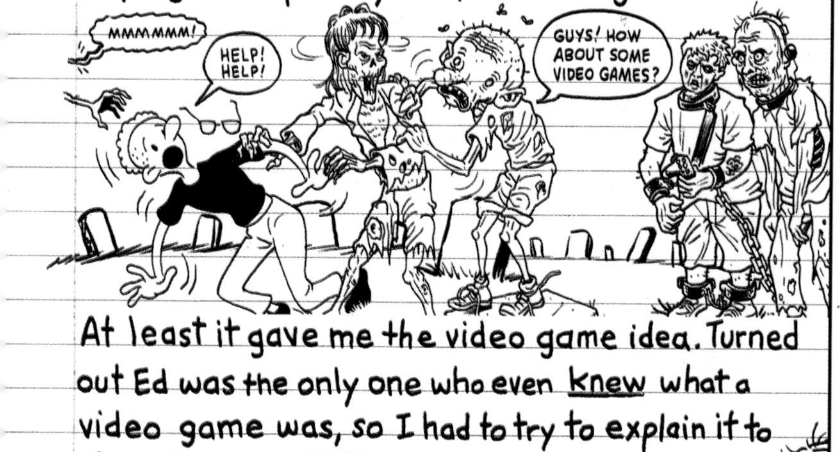
MMMMMMM!
HELP! HELP!
GUYS! HOW ABOUT SOME VIDEO GAMES?

At least it gave me the video game idea. Turned out Ed was the only one who even knew what a video game was, so I had to try to explain it to the others.

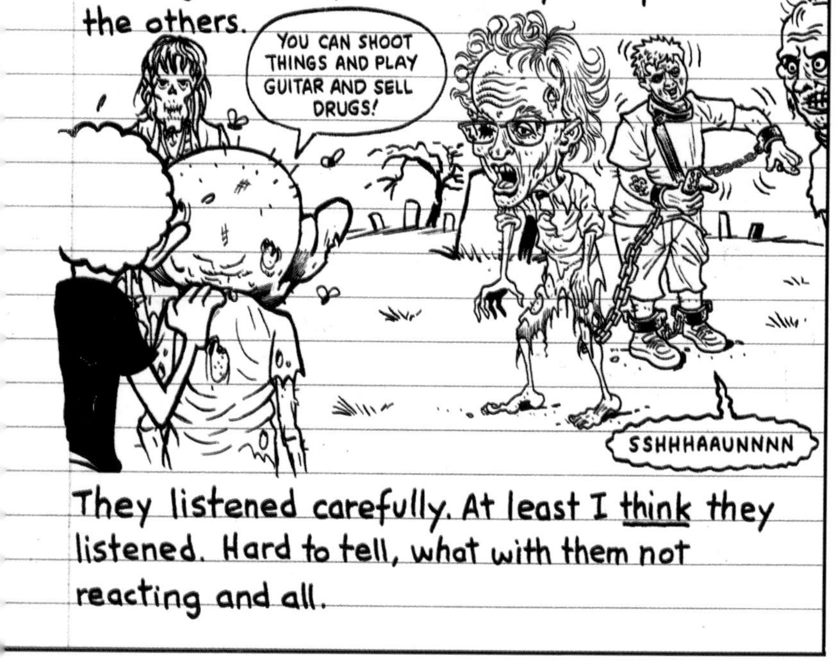
YOU CAN SHOOT THINGS AND PLAY GUITAR AND SELL DRUGS!
SSHHHAAUNNNN

They listened carefully. At least I think they listened. Hard to tell, what with them not reacting and all.

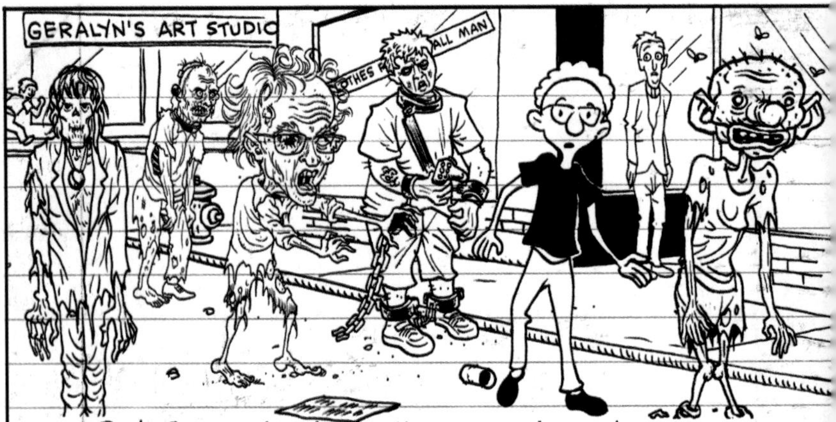
GERALYN'S ART STUDIO
ALL MAN

But I marched us all off for the video game store. I can't tell you how cool it was to strut down the street with my homies. I was starting to feel like I belonged!

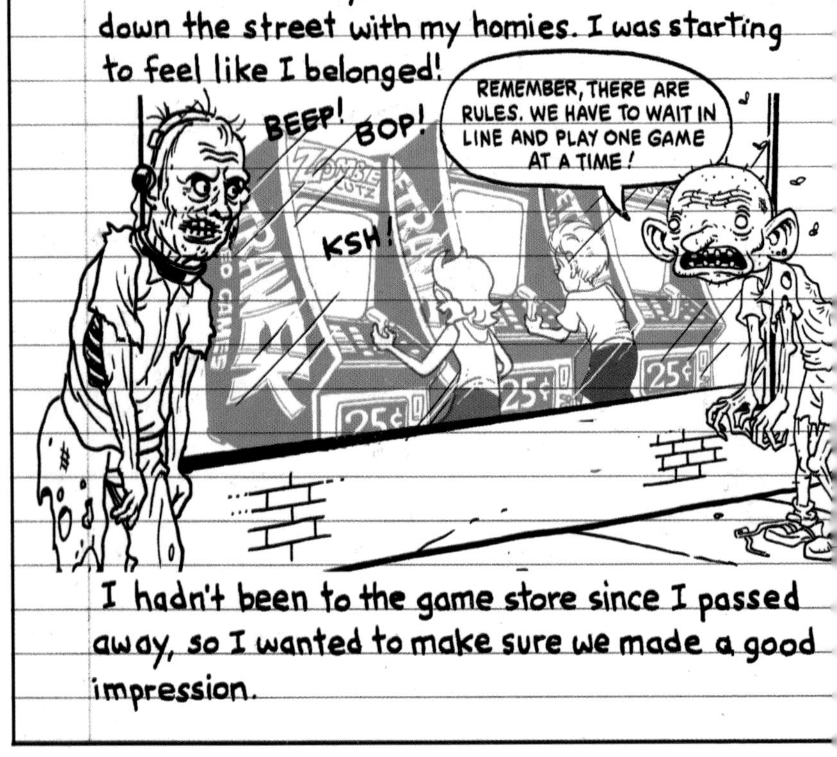
REMEMBER, THERE ARE RULES. WE HAVE TO WAIT IN LINE AND PLAY ONE GAME AT A TIME!
BEEP!
BOP!
KSH!
ZOMBIE
25¢
25¢
25¢

I hadn't been to the game store since I passed away, so I wanted to make sure we made a good impression.

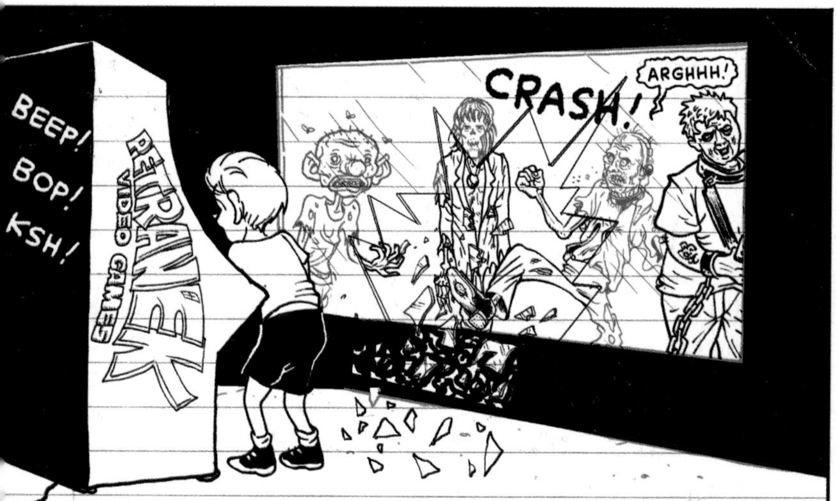
BEEP!
BOP!
KSH!
CRASH!
ARGHHH!

But the guys got a little EXCITED and jumped the gun. Everyone was so wrapped up in their gaming though, they barely noticed.

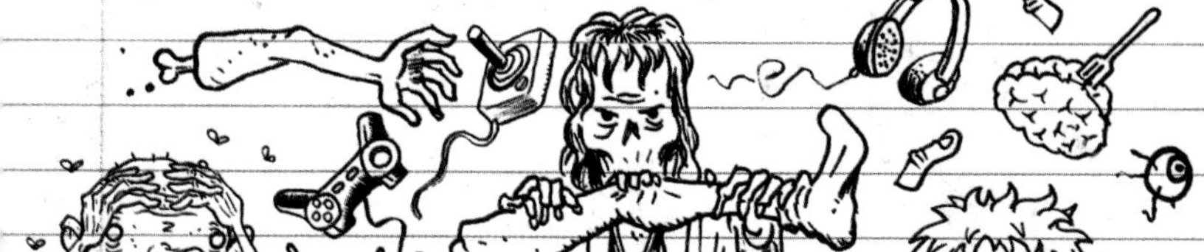

I guess my new pals WEREN'T listening. They totally ignored the ultra-cool games and started eating everybody. Even Ed was munching away. Talk about a snack attack!

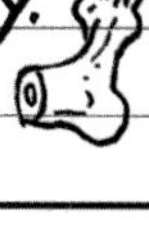

You'd think that snarfing down a store full of gamers would fill you up a little at least, but nope! No sooner were they finished, than they tried to eat Crowley again.

If Crowley was going to survive hanging with us, I'd have to do something. Z's aren't the brightest bulbs, so I figured I'd disguise him.

I pulled him aside, slapped a gamer's skull cap on him and told him it looked cool, even if it didn't. exactly fit. Then I gave him some pointers about playing dead.

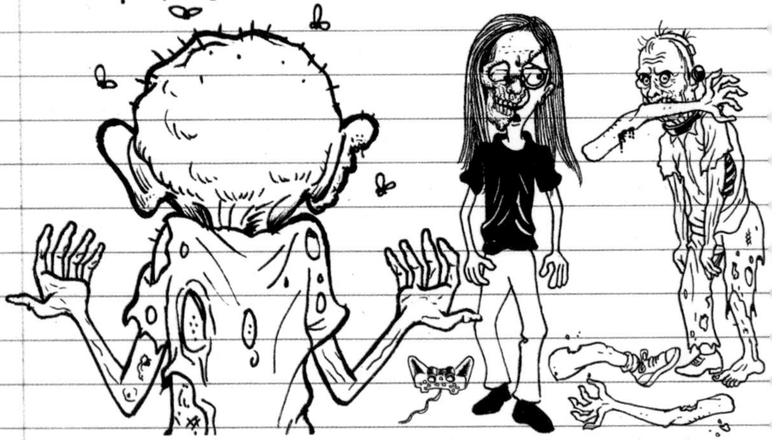

There was one other game store in town, in the mall. But they had the best game ever, GUITAR ZERO!

This time, I made sure things were clear. No eating, just fun! We waited, and of course, I went first, to demo my moves.

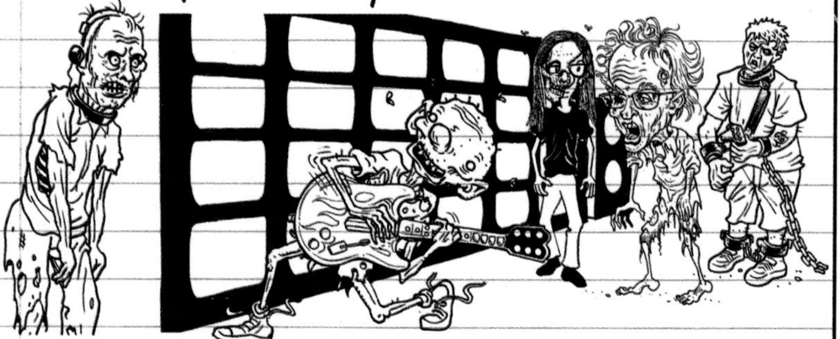

The gang was trying hard not to show it, but I KNOW I blew them away. Z's don't go for that heart-on-your-sleeve stuff, unless it falls through their chest and lands there, but inside, they're just, like big kids, all feeling.

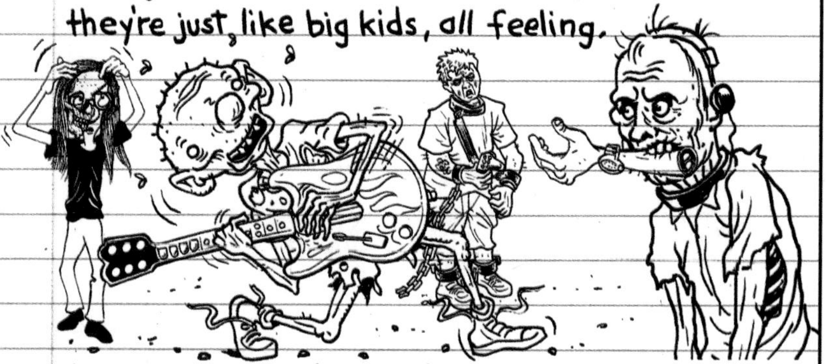

There was a little trouble because Bub was still gnawing on an arm from the other store, and there was a NO-SNACK sign, but the manager was cool about it. He just turned and ran.

After that, I figured the place was ours, but I hadn't counted on the human gamers standing their ground and waiting their turn. It was GUITAR ZERO after all, and I guess I was playing a little too long...

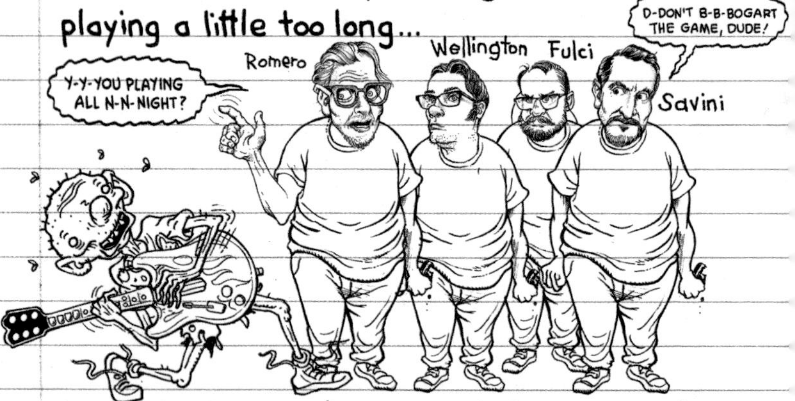
Y-Y-YOU PLAYING ALL N-N-NIGHT?
Romero
Wellington
Fulci
D-DON'T B-B-BOGART THE GAME, DUDE!
Savini

I wasn't totally cool with the `tude, but Bub took their gestures as a threat.

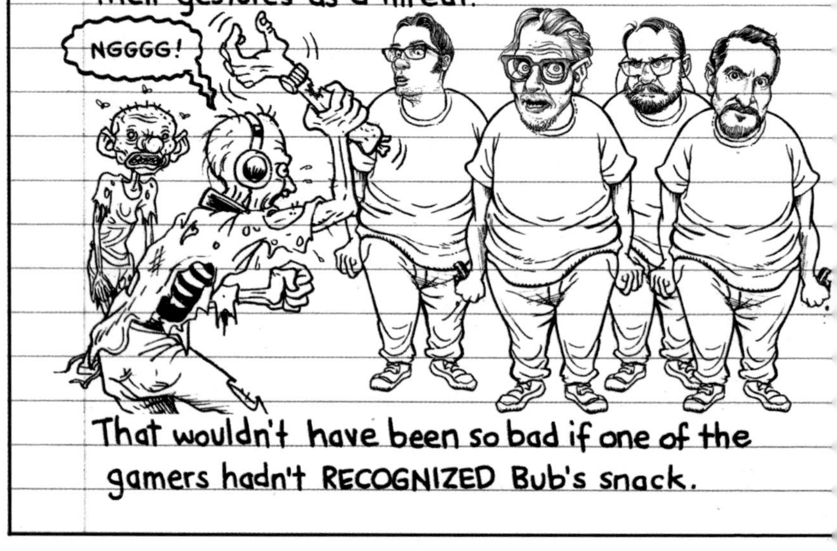
NGGGG!

That wouldn't have been so bad if one of the gamers hadn't RECOGNIZED Bub's snack.

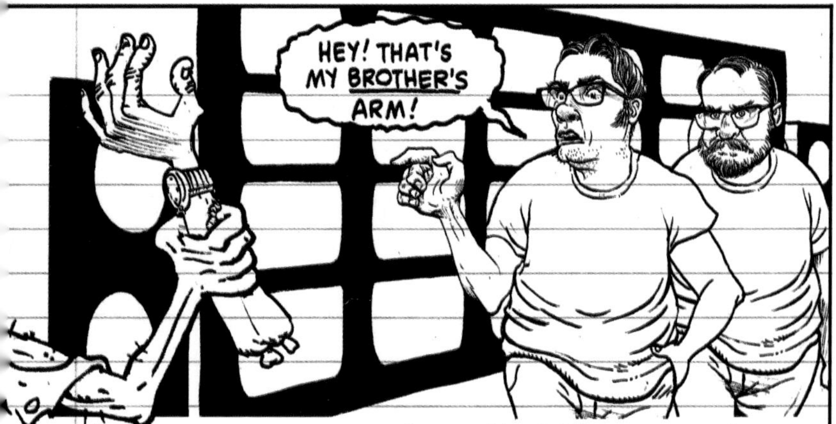
HEY! THAT'S MY BROTHER'S ARM!

As you might imagine, he got a little upset. They looked like they wanted to kill us.

Normally this wouldn't be a problem, but they'd played enough games to know ALL the ways to destroy Z's!

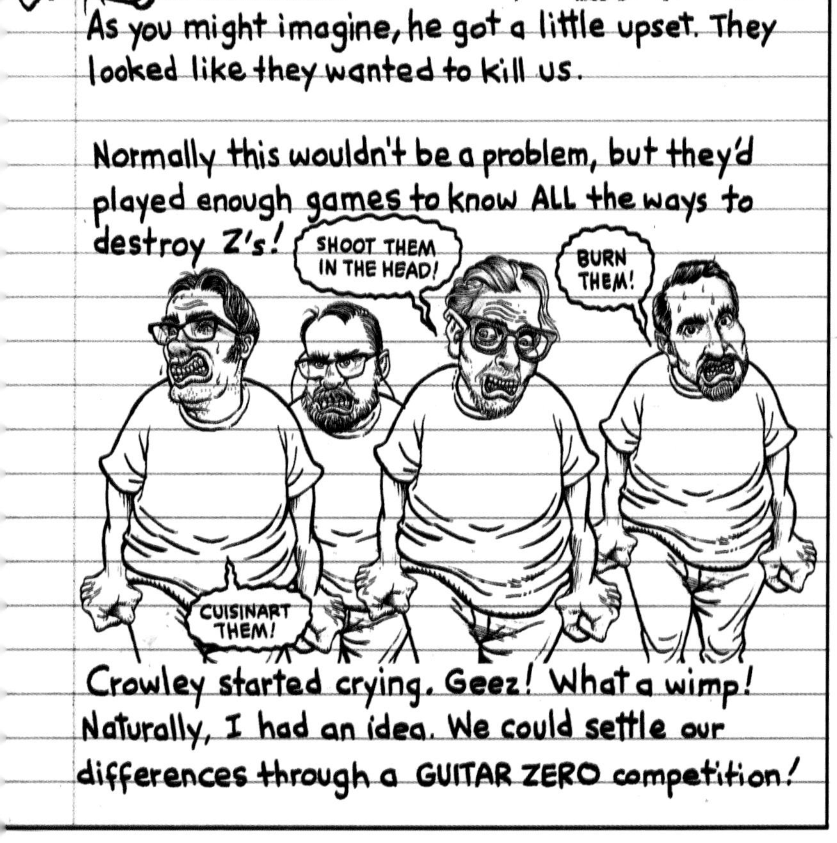
SHOOT THEM IN THE HEAD!
BURN THEM!
CUISINART THEM!

Crowley started crying. Geez! What a wimp! Naturally, I had an idea. We could settle our differences through a GUITAR ZERO competition!

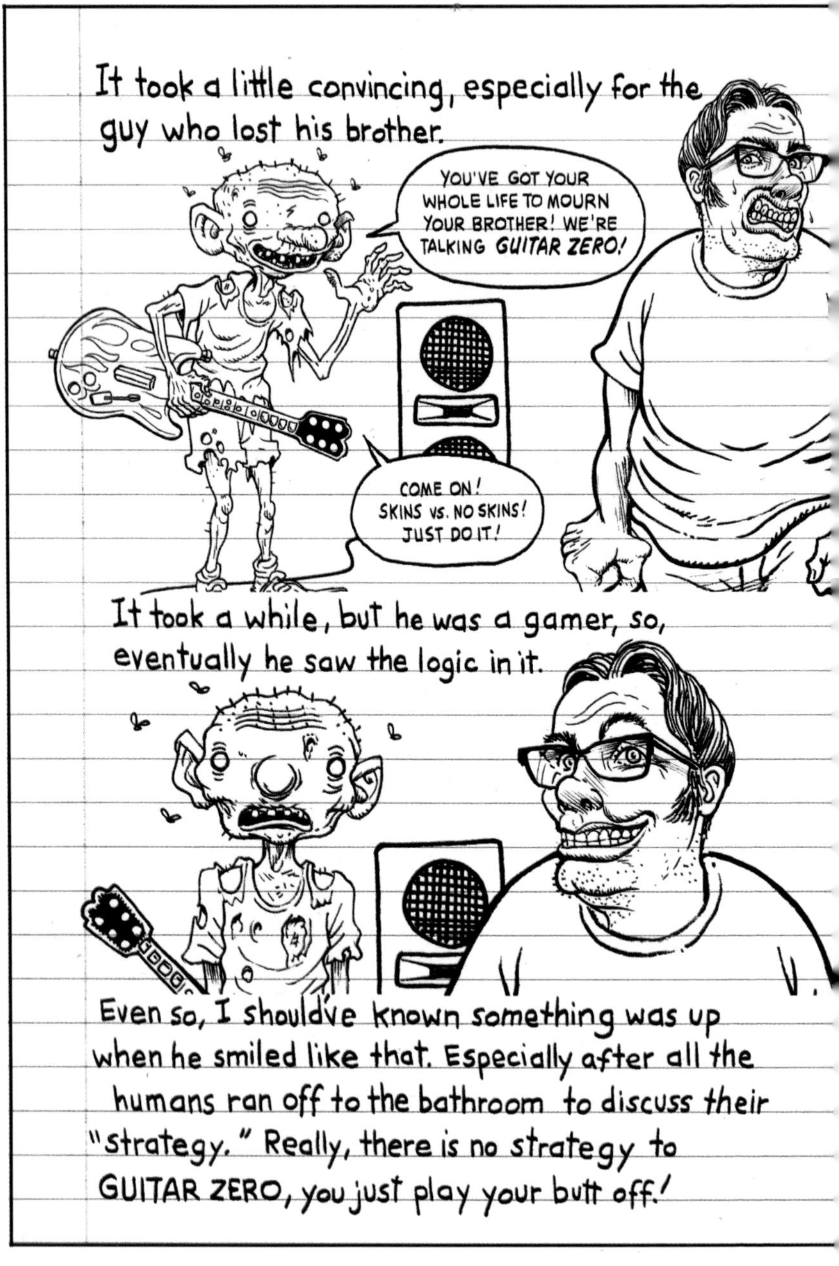
It took a little convincing, especially for the guy who lost his brother.
YOU'VE GOT YOUR WHOLE LIFE TO MOURN YOUR BROTHER! WE'RE TALKING GUITAR ZERO!
COME ON! SKINS VS. NO SKINS! JUST DO IT!
It took a while, but he was a gamer, so, eventually he saw the logic in it.
Even so, I should've known something was up when he smiled like that. Especially after all the humans ran off to the bathroom to discuss their "strategy." Really, there is no strategy to GUITAR ZERO, you just play your butt off!

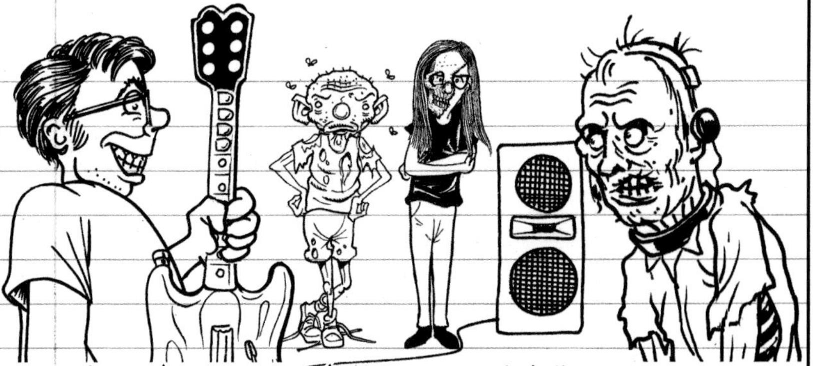

When they came out, they were totally confident, like they'd drank a case of Red Bull while they were in there or something.

After winning the skull toss (they called heads before I realized that was the *only* possibility), Wellington played first.

I figured the competition would be tough, but man, he was playing faster and better than that old sixties guitarist Jimi Hendrix! (Which made me wonder if we could get him here as a ringer...)

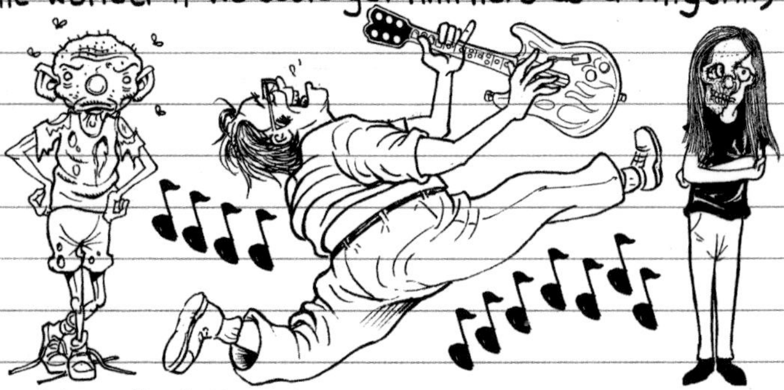

After that, it only got worse...

They were leaping all over, busting moves, hitting double scores, doing loop-de-loops!

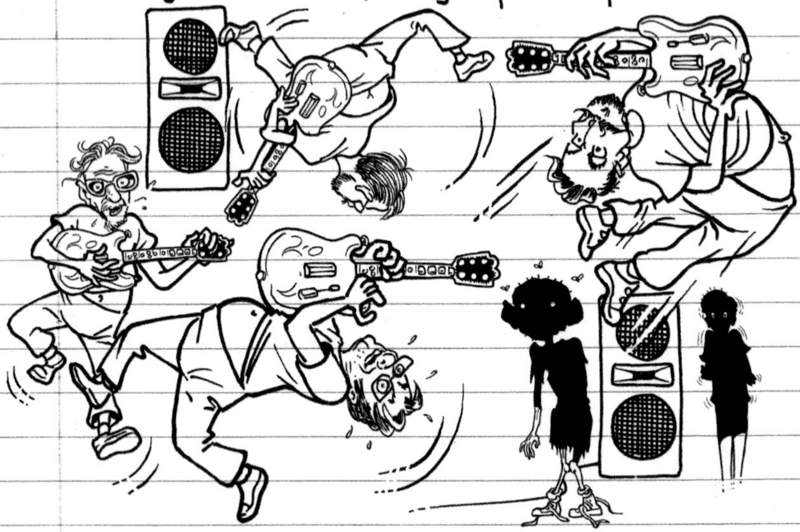

During the toughest solo in the game, Savini and Romero leapt up, slammed their chests into each other and played on each other's guitars!

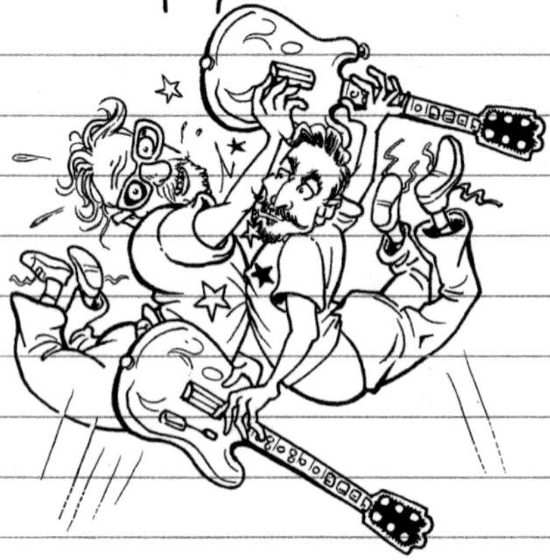

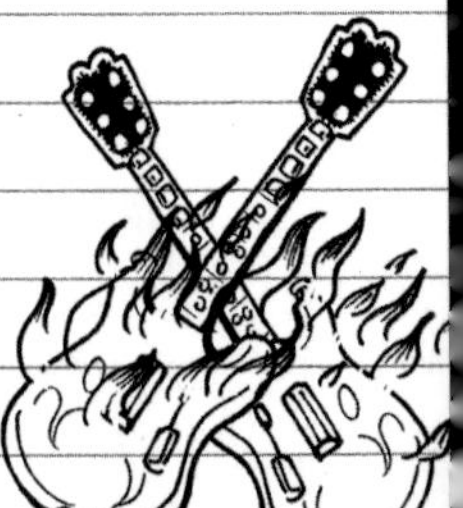

And their guitars burst into flames!

Then it was **OUR** turn.

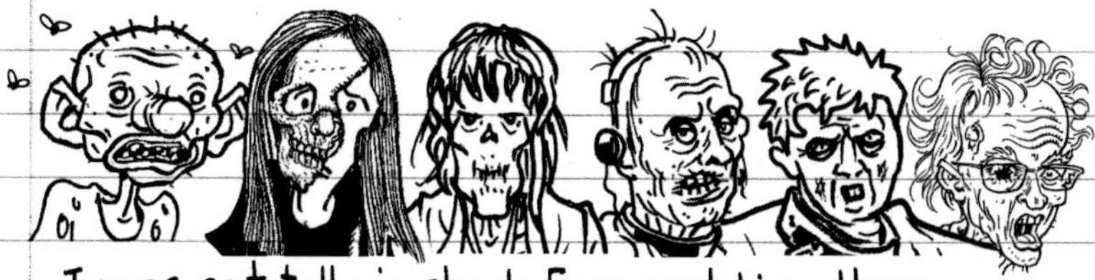

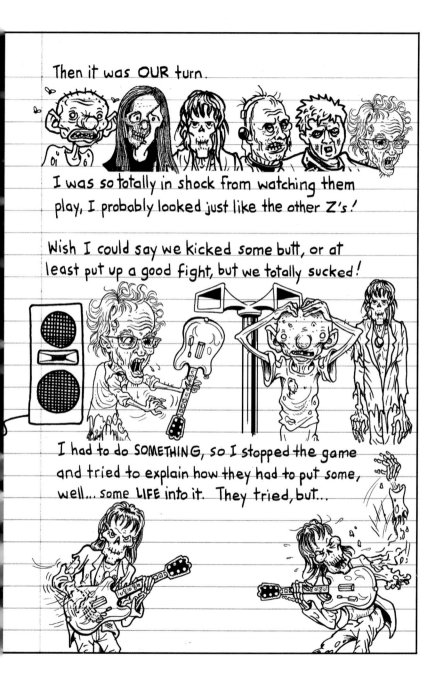

I was so totally in shock from watching them play, I probably looked just like the other Z's!

Wish I could say we kicked some butt, or at least put up a good fight, but we totally sucked!

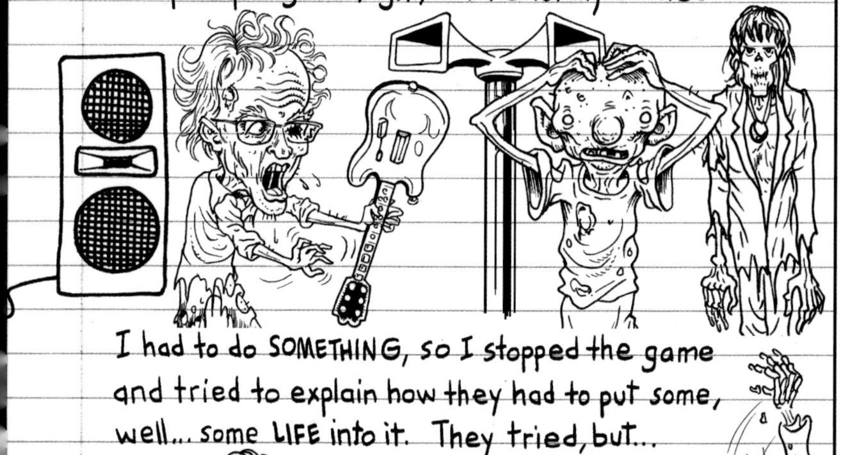

I had to do **SOMETHING**, so I stopped the game and tried to explain how they had to put some, well... some **LIFE** into it. They tried, but...

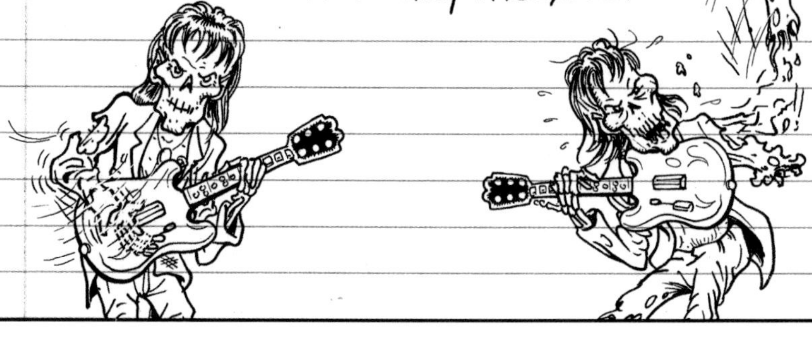

Bub and Boyle even made a go at leaping in the air and smashing chests.

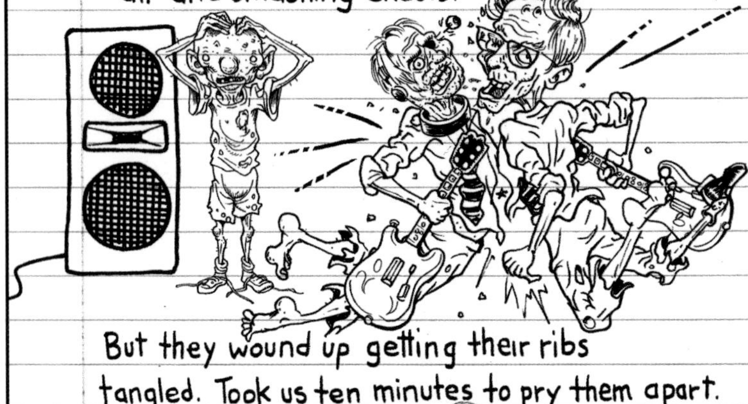

But they wound up getting their ribs tangled. Took us ten minutes to pry them apart.

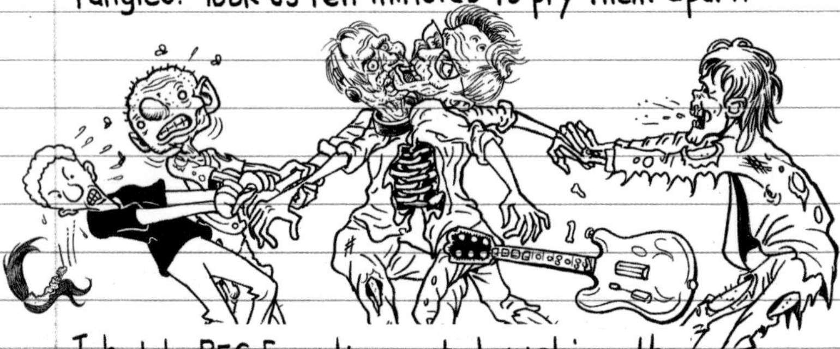

I had to BEG for a time out. Laughing, the gamers headed off for the bathroom again.

Crowley, meanwhile, not being a zombie, also had to go. I told him to be quick and he came back two seconds later, frantic.

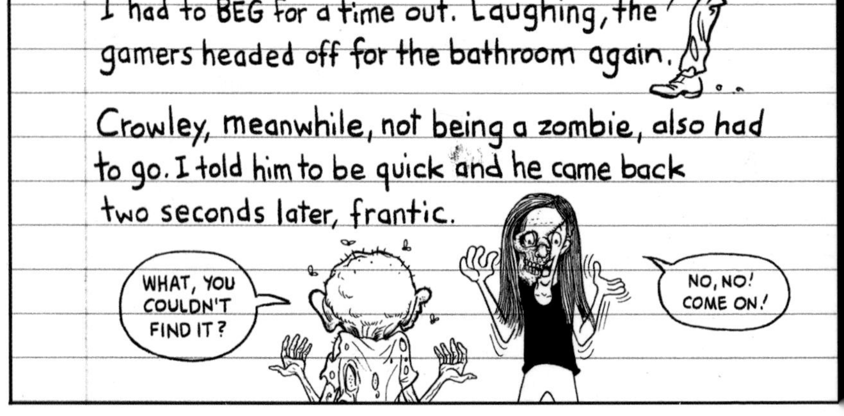
WHAT, YOU COULDN'T FIND IT?
NO, NO! COME ON!

You wouldn't believe it. I mean, I didn't believe it and I was looking right at it!

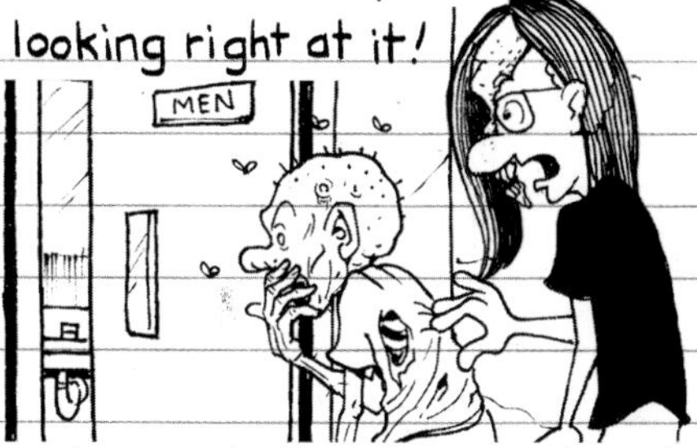
MEN

The gamers were talking to the demon Nixus! I guess he'd gotten pretty bored himself since my Mom kicked him out of our basement.

Wellington and those creeps made a demonic DEAL to beat our butts! If they won, Nixus would not only get our souls, they'd get a copy of GUITAR ZERO II: FROM ZERO TO HELL and it wasn't even out yet!

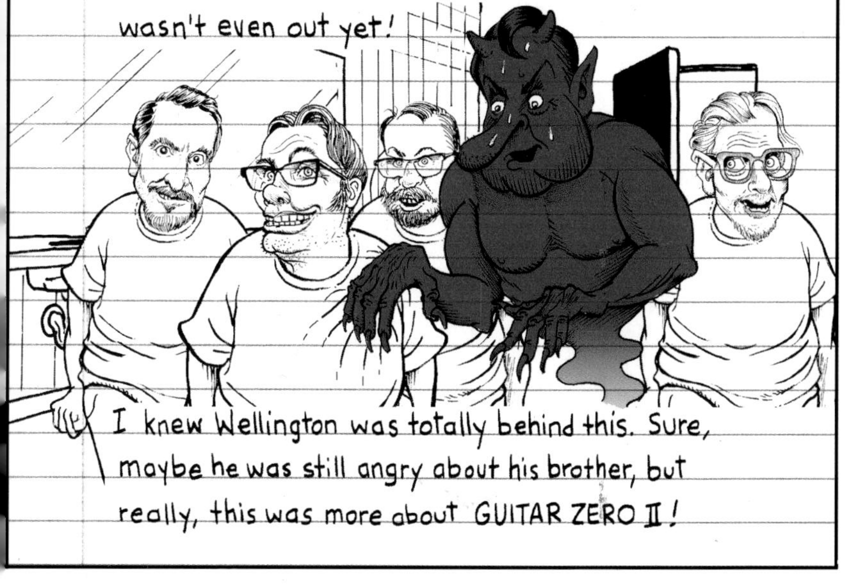

I knew Wellington was totally behind this. Sure, maybe he was still angry about his brother, but really, this was more about GUITAR ZERO II!

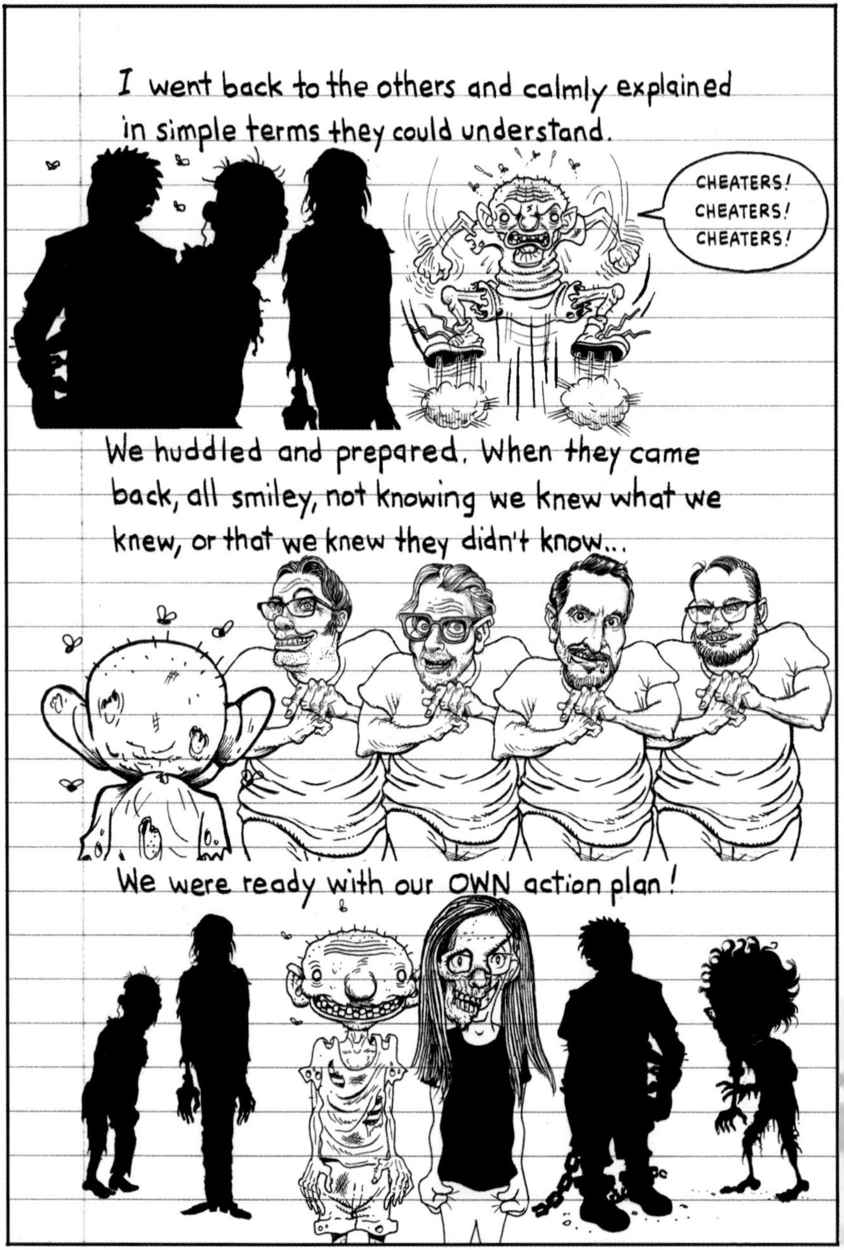
I went back to the others and calmly explained in simple terms they could understand.
CHEATERS! CHEATERS! CHEATERS!
We huddled and prepared. When they came back, all smiley, not knowing we knew what we knew, or that we knew they didn't know...
We were ready with our OWN action plan!

We ate them! We couldn't BEAT them, right?

MUNCH!
MUNCH!

Even Crowley had a piece! He insisted he wasn't becoming a cannibal or anything, but these guys just weren't playing fair!

You have to admire the man's sense of justice.

Unfortunately, the last laugh was on us! Nixus was totally P.O.'d. In a final act of really picky and totally unfair spite, he cursed us so that every person we ever killed came back as a Z.

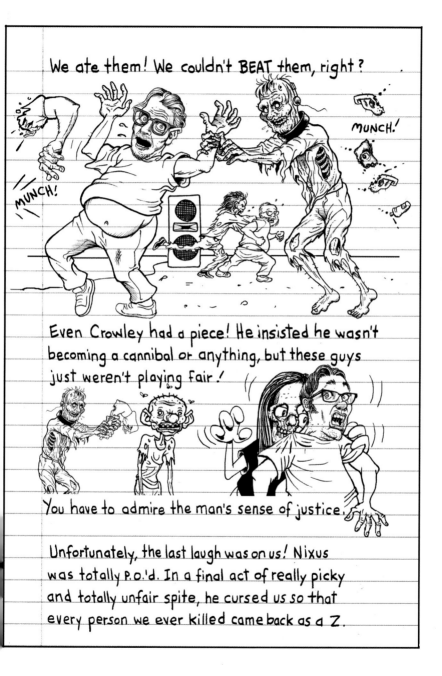

Now the cemetery's packed like our old school bus and the SMELL is ten times worse!

I'm thinking of suggesting a game of football, heads versus no-heads. Wonder if they'll buy that. Plus, we'd need a foot.

Crowley still complains about how everyone wants to eat him, but I told him to lighten up. Who wants to live forever anyway?

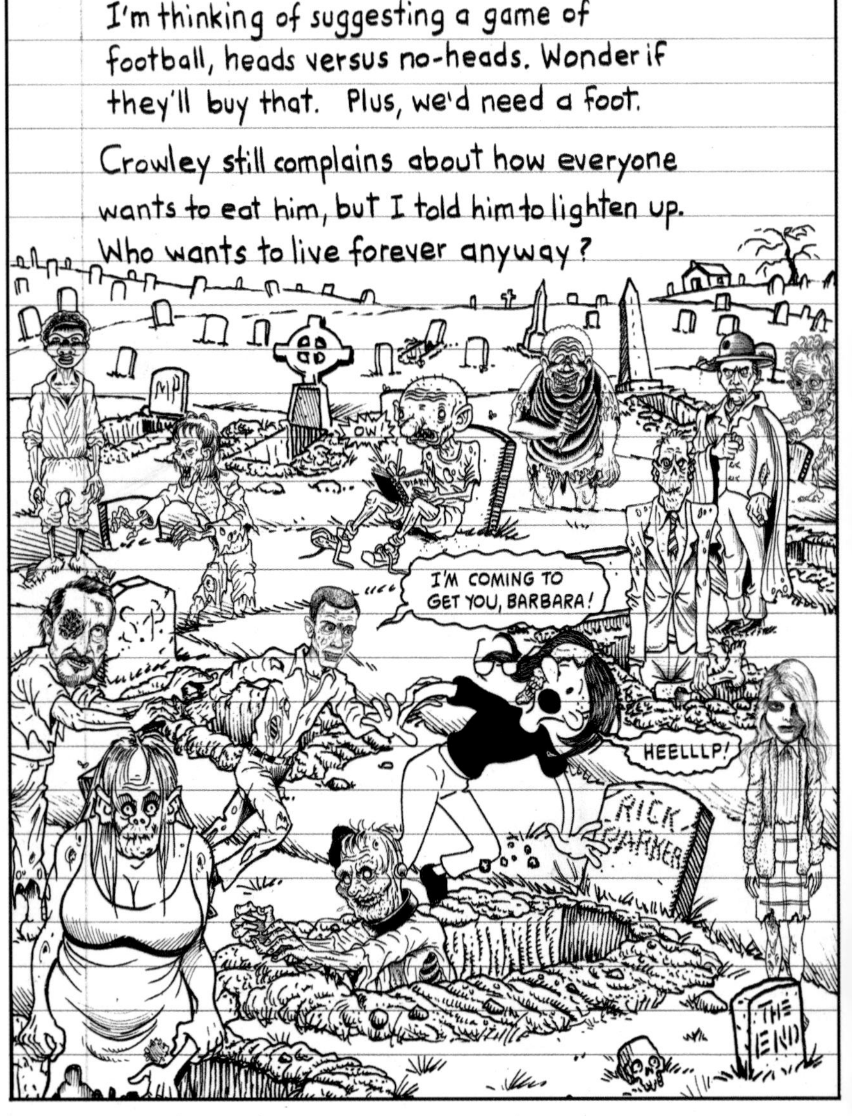

OW!
DIARY
I'M COMING TO GET YOU, BARBARA!
HEELLLP!
RICK PARKER
THE END

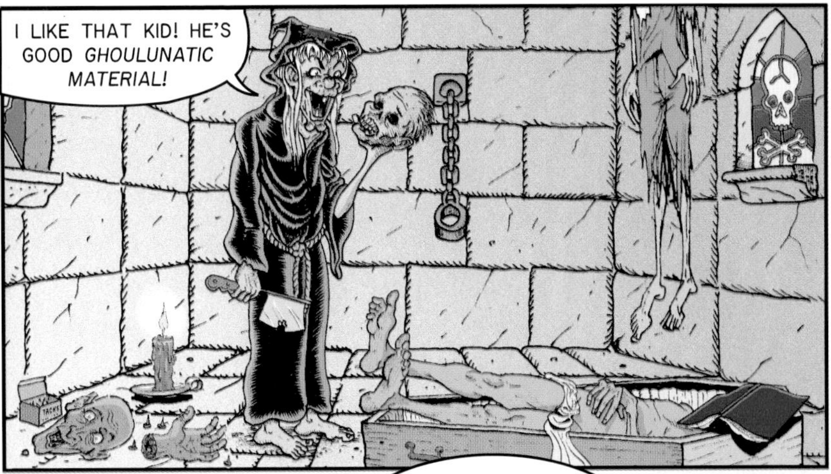
I LIKE THAT KID! HE'S GOOD *GHOULUNATIC* *MATERIAL!*
TACKS

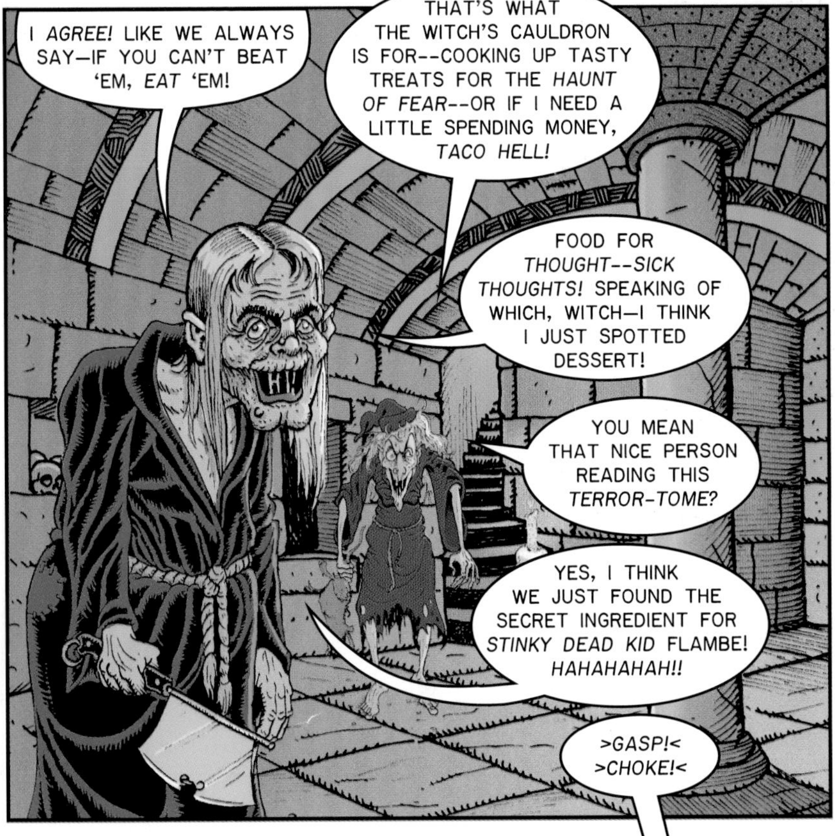
I *AGREE!* LIKE WE ALWAYS SAY—IF YOU CAN'T BEAT 'EM, *EAT* 'EM!
THAT'S WHAT THE WITCH'S CAULDRON IS FOR--COOKING UP TASTY TREATS FOR THE *HAUNT OF FEAR*--OR IF I NEED A LITTLE SPENDING MONEY, *TACO HELL!*
FOOD FOR *THOUGHT--SICK THOUGHTS!* SPEAKING OF WHICH, WITCH—I THINK I JUST SPOTTED DESSERT!
YOU MEAN THAT NICE PERSON READING THIS *TERROR-TOME?*
YES, I THINK WE JUST FOUND THE SECRET INGREDIENT FOR *STINKY DEAD KID* FLAMBE! *HAHAHAHAH!!*
>GASP!<
>CHOKE!<

THE HARDY BOYS

A NEW GRAPHIC NOVEL EVERY 3 MONTHS!

#14 "Haley Danielle's Top Eight!"
ISBN – 978-1-59707-113-0
#15 "Live Free, Die Hardy!"
ISBN – 978-1-59707-123-9
#16 "SHHHHHH!"
ISBN – 978-1-59707-138-3
#17 "Word Up!"
ISBN – 978-1-59707-147-5
NEW! **#18 "D.A.N.G.E.R. Spells The Hangman!"**
ISBN – 978-1-59707-160-4
Also available – Hardy Boys #1-13
All: Pocket sized, 96-112 pp., full-color, $7.95
Also available in hardcover! $12.95

NEW!

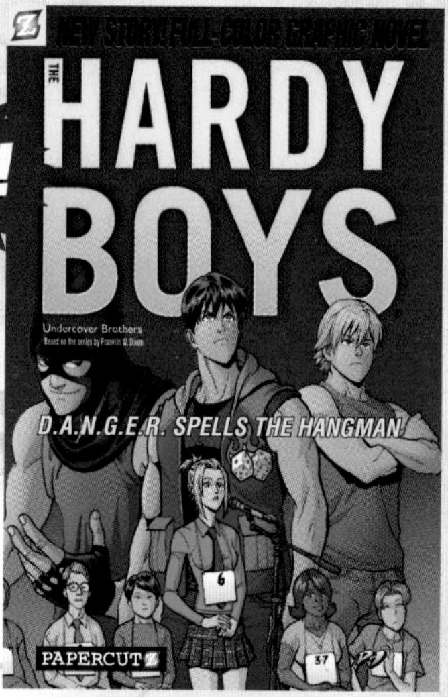
NEW STORY! FULL-COLOR GRAPHIC NOVEL
THE
HARDY
BOYS
Undercover Brothers
D.A.N.G.E.R. SPELLS THE HANGMAN
PAPERCUTZ

THE HARDY BOYS BOXED SETS
#1-4 ISBN – 978-1-59707-040-9
#5-8 ISBN – 978-1-59707-075-1
#9-12 ISBN – 978-1-59707-125-3
#13-16 ISBN – 978-1-59707-173-4
All: Full-color, $29.95

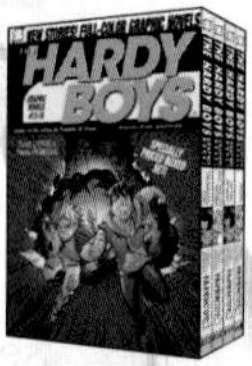
HARDY
BOYS

CLASSICS *Illustrated*
Featuring Stories by the World's Greatest Authors

#1 "Great Expectations"
ISBN - 978-1-59707-097-3
#2 "The Invisible Man"
ISBN - 978-1-59707-106-2
#3 "Through the Looking-Glass"
ISBN - 978-1-59707-115-4
#4 "The Raven and Other Poems"
ISBN - 978-1-59707-140-6
#5 "Hamlet"
ISBN - 978-1-59707-149-9
NEW! **#6 "The Scarlet Letter"**
ISBN - 978-1-59707-162-8
All: 6 1/2 x 9, 56 pp., full-color, $9.95, hardcover

NEW!

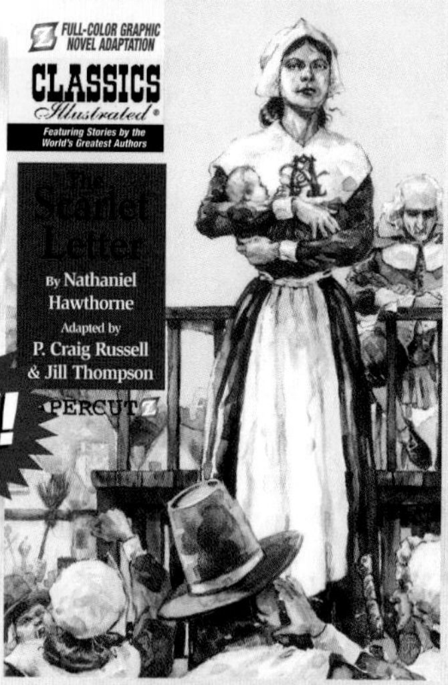
FULL-COLOR GRAPHIC NOVEL ADAPTATION
CLASSICS
Illustrated
Featuring Stories by the World's Greatest Authors
The Scarlet Letter
By Nathaniel Hawthorne
Adapted by
P. Craig Russell
& Jill Thompson
PAPERCUTZ

ON SALE AT BOOKSTORES EVERYWHERE!

Please add $4.00 postage and handling. Add $1.00 for each additional item.
Make check payable to NBM publishing. Send To:
Papercutz, 40 Exchange Place, Suite 1308,
New York, New York 10005, 1-800-886-1223
www.papercutz.com

WATCH OUT FOR PAPERCUTZ™

Jim Salicrup, The Old Editor, here to welcome you to the Papercutz Backpages and to deliver a very important message. If you've enjoyed what we've been doing in the Papercutz version of TALES FROM THE CRYPT, we need your help. It seems that the revival of TALES FROM THE CRYPT may be the best-kept secret in the world of publishing, and while we have a wonderful loyal following, we need even more faithful followers if we're to continue creating all-new CRYPTy goodness. So, in this Internet Age of super connectedness, it would be great if each and everyone of you reach out to all your online friends (and enemies too!) and let them know how much you enjoyed TALES FROM THE CRYPT #8 "Diary of a Stinky Dead Kid"! You can mention that there's also "DieLite" – a sappy vampire love story for people who hate sappy vampire love stories, and "Carrier"— a sequel to CRYPT #7's "Night Traveler" and the best werewolf/trucker story we've ever seen!

For those of you just joining us, there's still time to catch up on all the previous terror-filled tales! On the following pages we point out that TALES FROM THE CRYPT has been combining horror with humor since the very beginning. (Remember, each previous volume is still available from us, or your favorite bookseller. If any booksellers are out of stock, they can certainly order it for you!) Whether it's poisonous parodies or just sick, gross humor in the TALES FROM THE CRYPT tradition, the Papercutz incarnation of EC's premier horror-comicbook loves to make you laugh one minute and scream the next!

For further laughs and screams be sure to visit us at www.papercutz.com and check out the Papercutz Blog for more news on TALES FROM THE CRYPT, as well as BIONICLE, CLASSICS ILLUSTRATED, DISNEY FAIRIES, GERONIMO STILTON, THE HARDY BOYS, NANCY DREW, and every other Papercutz graphic novel series. So, let's wrap up with (Gasp!) a picture (Choke!) of Yours Truly, as I thank you all for your continued support!

Thanks,

Jim

THE OLD EDITOR

Caricature by Rick Parker.

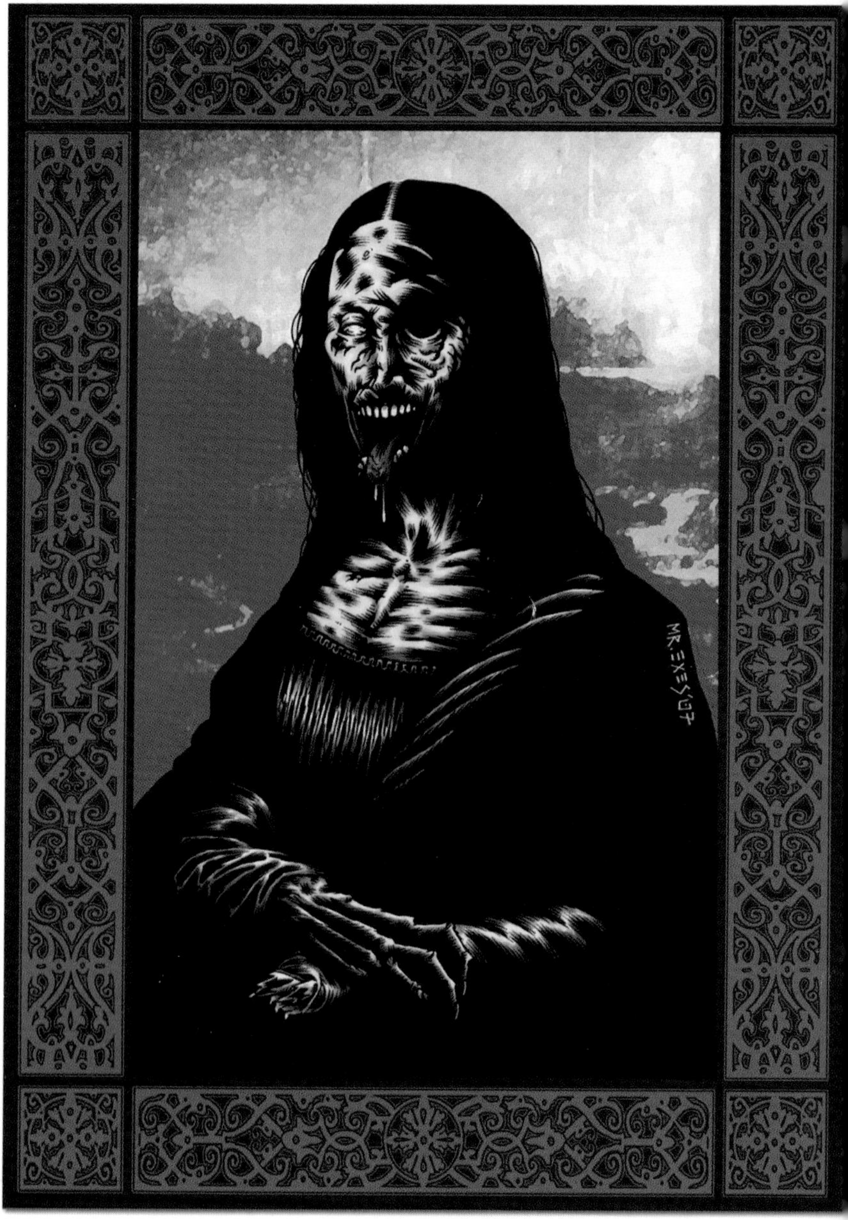

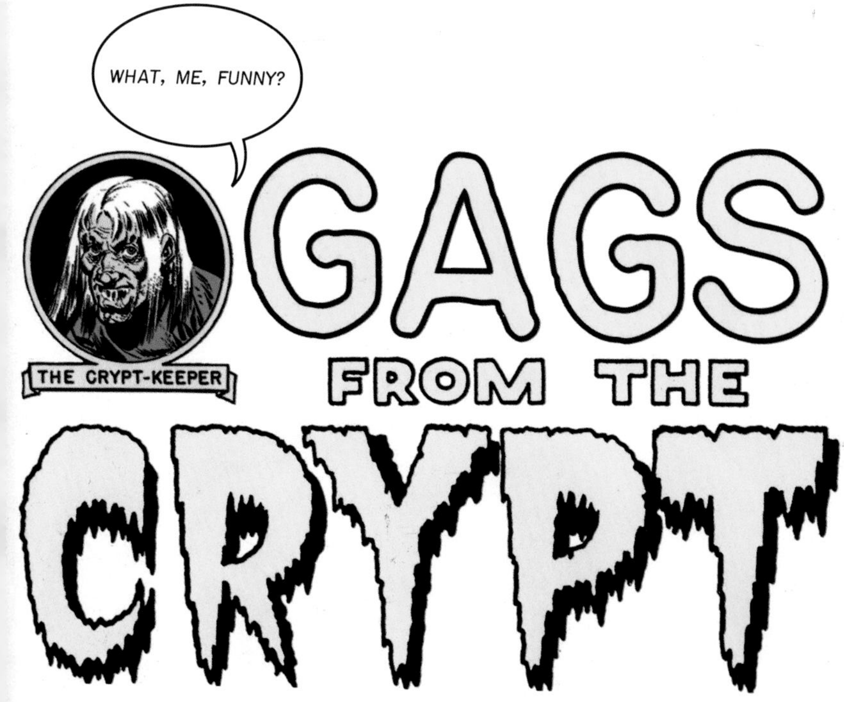
WHAT, ME, FUNNY?
THE CRYPT-KEEPER

GAGS FROM THE CRYPT

There's always been a very strong connection between horror and humor, especially with Gallows Humor and Black Humor. Many of the original TALES FROM THE CRYPT stories from the classic 50s EC comic have been described as gloriously illustrated sick jokes. The gross, over-the-top punch lines – or "shock endings" -- were a big part of the of the comic's appeal. So, when Papercutz revived TALES FROM THE CRYPT, humor was always a part of the new series. Just look at the zombie-fied version of the Mona Lisa that was cover featured on the premiere Papercutz volume, entitled "Ghouls Gone Wild!"

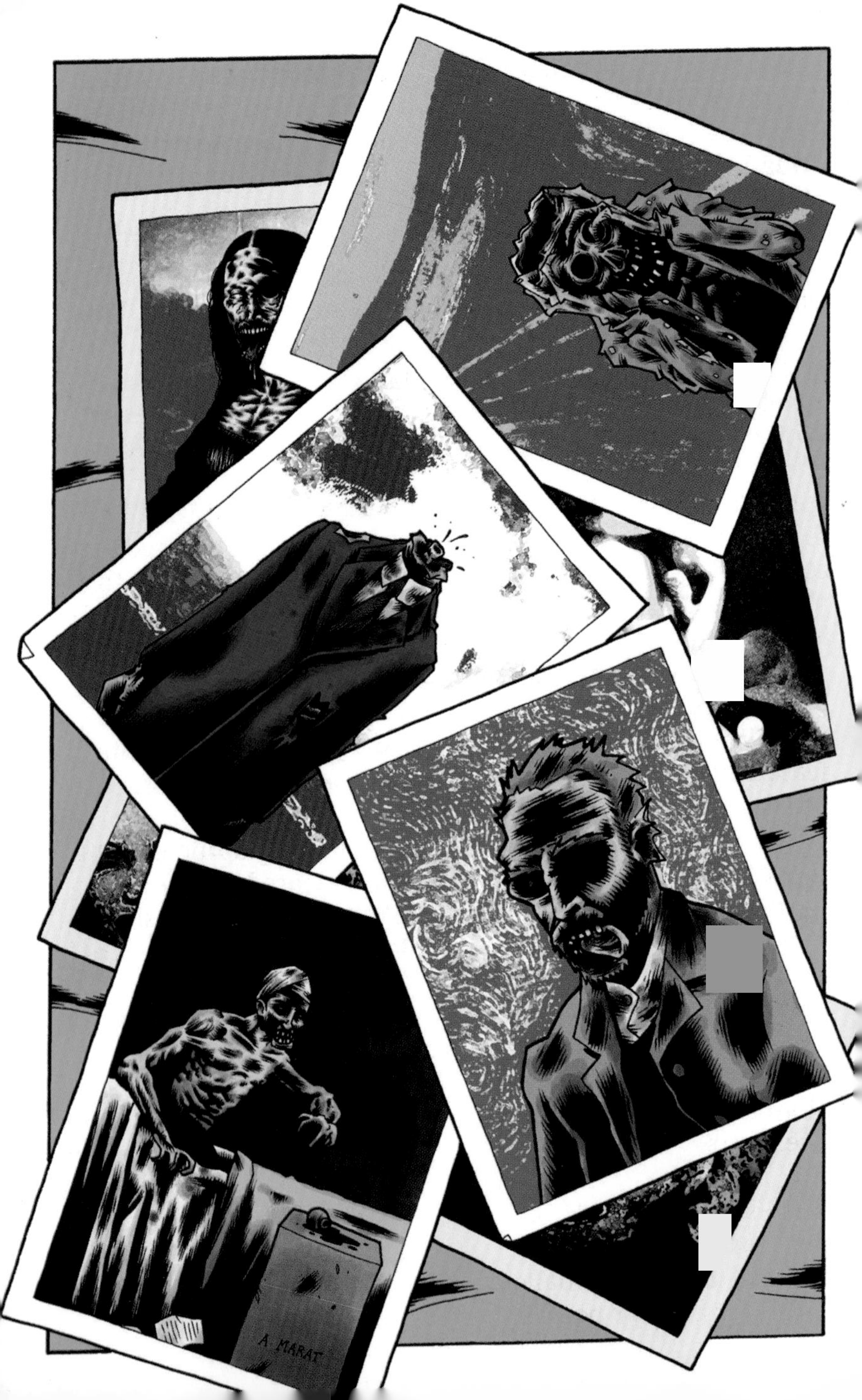
A MARAT

We also met Pop Artist Jack Kroll in TALES FROM THE CRYPT #1. Kroll, who kinda looks like Andy Warhol, moves next door to Mike and Linda Anderson in Cranwell, New Jersey, and the Andersons soon see stealing Kroll's original artworks as their ticket out of suburbia. While "Body of Work" by Marc Bilgrey and Mr. Exes seems like a typical tale in the CRYPT tradition, the zombie-fied art masterpieces by Kroll are truly inspired! It's this same type of humor that spawned the best-selling "Pride and Prejudice and Zombies," featuring the original text of Jane Austen's classic novel with all-new added scenes of zombies. Even more shocking is the real-life art exhibit that features real human corpses called "Bodies," that has become a huge success. That's creepier and funnier than anything we could dream up!

Also in CRYPT #1, in "Serious Collectors Only" we met Thomas Donalley, a collector of fully-poseable, micro-articulated action figures. Thomas gave writer Rob Vollmar and artist Tim Smith 3 the opportunity to have fun with the stereotype of today's modern comicbook fan -- a guy with a dead-end job living in his mother's basement. We must've really liked Thomas as he returned in CRYPT #3 in "Graveyard Shift at the Twilight Gardens" where he found employment at an old age home, and attempted to steal from its resident vampire. And again in CRYPT #6 in "Brain Food," where Thomas is finally institutionalized and encounters a brain-eating monster.

CRYPT graphic novel #1 also featured a Will Eisner-like take on an evil slumlord entitled "The Tenant" by Neil Kleid and Steve Mannion. But the most outright parody was "Runway Roadkill" by Don McGregor and Sho Murase -- a terror-filled take-off on "The Devil Wears Prada," a story that gives new meaning to the phrase "fashion victim."

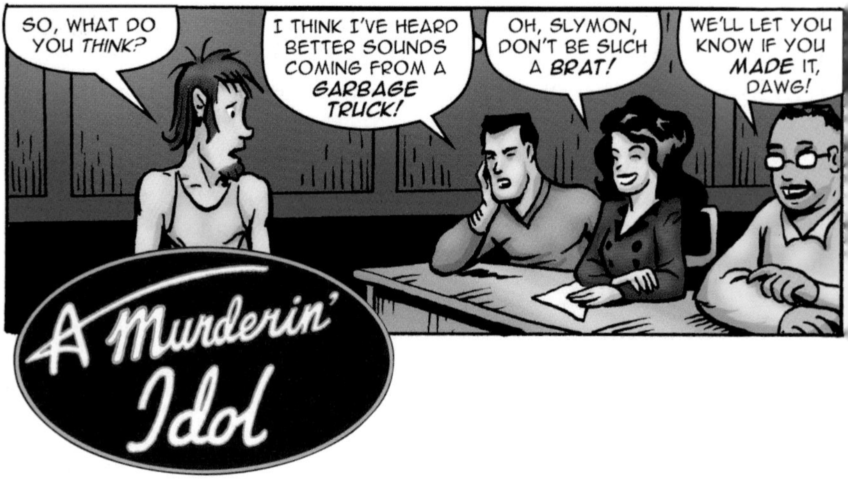
SO, WHAT DO YOU THINK?
I THINK I'VE HEARD BETTER SOUNDS COMING FROM A GARBAGE TRUCK!
OH, SLYMON, DON'T BE SUCH A BRAT!
WE'LL LET YOU KNOW IF YOU MADE IT, DAWG!
A Murderin' Idol

The point we're making is simply that humor has been part of TALES FROM THE CRYPT from the start -- from the original classic EC Comics to the HBO series right up to the Papercutz version. Mort Todd, one-time editor of CRACKED magazine concocted "A Murderin' Idol," illustrated by Steve Mannion, for TALES FROM THE CRYPT #2. Obviously inspired by the hit TV talent contest that is still tops in the ratings. CRYPT #2's title "Can You Fear Me Now?" is itself a take-off on the advertising slogan of a major wireless phone company, and was inspired by "Crystal Clear," by Don McGregor and James Romberger, the tale of a drug dealer with a phone implanted in his head. "Slabbed!" by Stefan Petrucha and Don Hudson takes aim at comicbook collectors in this satirical shocker. "The Garden" by Fred Van Lente and Mr. Exes, tackles an issue torn from today's headlines, with a powerful twist ending in the true EC tradition.

TALES FROM THE CRYPT #3 "Zombielicious"!" continued along the same lines—"Extra Life" by Neil Kleid and Chris Noeth explored the potential consequences of a life lived online in a never-ending war game. "Queen of the Vampires" by Marc Bilgrey and Mr. Exes hammered the last nail into the coffin of prissy Goth vampires and their fans and creators. "Kid Tested, Mother Approved" by Jared Gnewek and James Romberger offered a truly biting satire on the food we eat, especially for breakfast.

TALES FROM THE CRYPT #4 "Crypt-Keeping It Real" offered lots of traditional horror stories, but introduced a few shorter tales via "You Toomb" and "Jumping the Shark" by MAD writer Ari Kaplan and Mr. Exes, took a satirical swipe at TV in general and "reality" shows in particular.

TALES FROM THE CRYPT #5 "Yabba dabba Voodoo" continued the trend toward darker stories, but as disgusting as "Ignoble Rot" by Fred Van Lente and Mort Todd was, you'd be hard-pressed not to laugh at the pitiful protagonist's putrid plight.

TALES FROM THE CRYPT #6 "You Toomb" also is filled with less satire and more dark humor, but the stories found in this volume are some of the finest, particulary if you enjoy baby vampires, voodoo hitmen, and killer robots.

TALES FROM THE CRYPT #7 "Something Wicca This

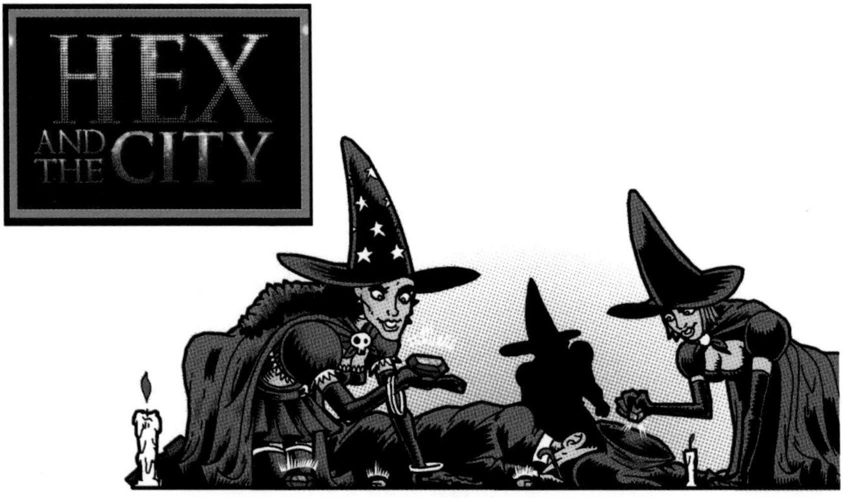
HEX
AND THE CITY

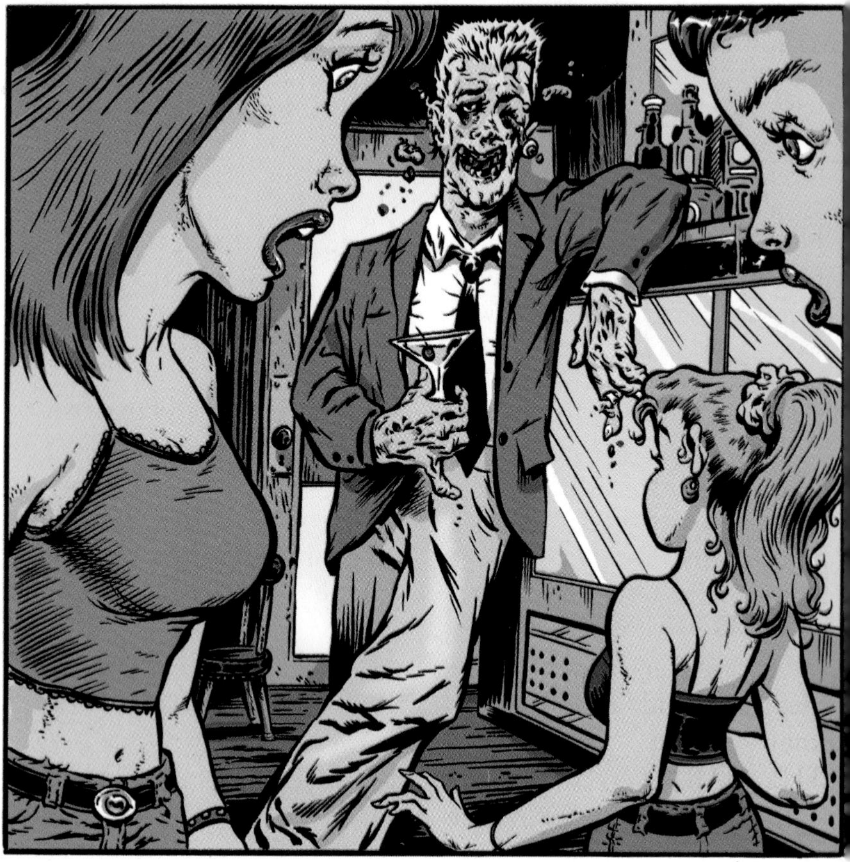

Way Comes" marked the return of parody in a big way—the tale of the three sexy New York City career women who resort to witchcraft to kill their new boss in "Hex and the City" by Stefan Petrucha and Mr. Exes prompted the "WITCHMAN" cover on the paperback editions. And to further prove how humor was always a CRYPT staple, we presented "Lower Berth" an EC CRYPT classic by Al Feldstein and Jack Davis.

Which brings us to our current volume, crammed with take-offs of two of today's most popular book series. Being CRYPT we just had to kill that Kid and destroy that vampire. It's just how we are. We can't help it. It's tradition. One we hope continues—with your loyal support.

MEET HARDY BOYS GRAPHIC NOVELS ARTIST “PH”-

PAULO HENRIQUE!

A **PAPERCUTZ**™ PROFILE

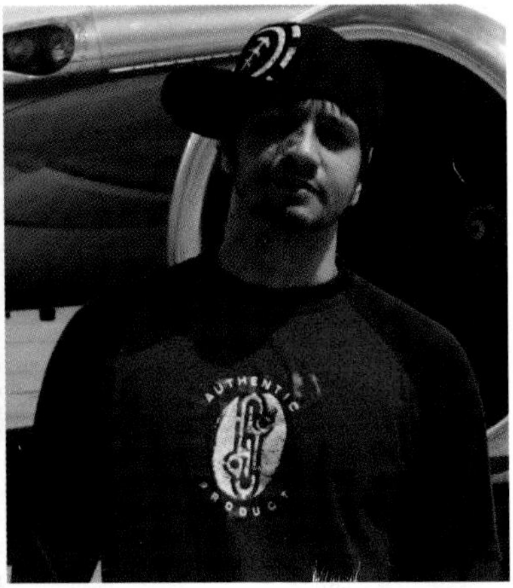

Hi there, my name is Paulo Henrique and most of you know me as the artist of THE HARDY BOYS Graphic Novels for Papercutz. One thing you might not know is that I prefer to go by “PH” instead of “Paulo Henrique.” I'd like to share a bit about myself and let you all ask any questions you may have for me over on the Papercutz Blog (go to www.papercutz.com). I always like to hear from fans.

I was born in Sao Paulo, Brazil where I started drawing at a very young age. The first thing I remember drawing was from when I was 6 years old. I was in art class and I drew a picture of Darth Vader – the villain from STAR WARS. The teacher said she thought that I had drawn a bride in a black wedding dress! I always liked bad guys the best, but I knew that Vader was a good guy under that mask. That's why I liked him so much as a kid.

After that, I just kept on drawing and drawing. I really like “larger than life” characters, and when I was growing up I was drawn to Manga-style art before I even knew that's what it was called. Manga is actually the Japanese word for comics, but there are many unique elements of this Japanese art style that we use in THE HARDY BOYS a lot. An easy way to identify the style is characters with cartoonishly exaggerated faces and bodies. If you want a good example of some Manga-esque HARDY BOYS, look at the fourth page of comics in THE HARDY BOYS Graphic Novel #14

"Haley Danielle's Top Eight!":

Some of the best-known artists who shaped what we know as Manga today are Machiko Hasegawa and Osamu Tezuka. You have probably seen Tezuka's "Astro Boy" at some point in your life. Google it! The history of Manga goes all the way back to the 1800's and there's a lot of info on the Internet if you do some searching.

Back to my art! Some of you may want to know who my favorite comics characters are and how I got started. Well, I love that Blue Bomber! I'm talking about Megaman. I started drawing him when I was a teenager and I've beaten all of the original Nintendo games. Megaman is a Manga character and he jump-started my career. In 1997, I was hired to draw the MEGAMAN comicbook for Brazilian publisher Magnum and ended up working with Sidney Lima, who would work on ZORRO and THE HARDY BOYS at Papercutz years later. At that time, a lot of publishers got interested in Manga, so I met with Magnum and did a test for Megaman. Both Sidney Lima and I ended up getting the job, and we became friends.

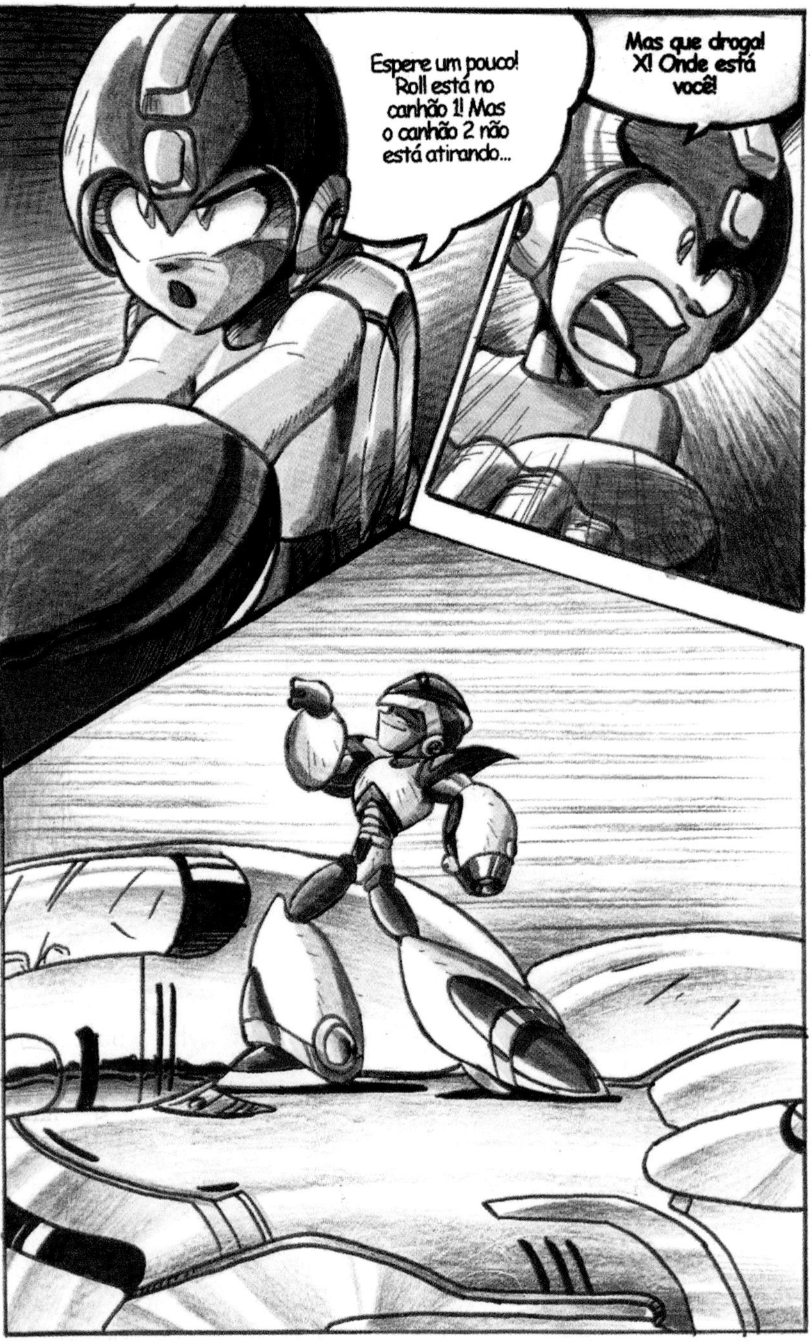
Espere um pouco! Roll está no canhão 1! Mas o canhão 2 não está atirando...
Mas que droga! X! Onde está você!

Years later I started to work for Yabu Media and was doing an electronic graphic novel called COMBO RANGERS, so I called him to work with me. This led to us collaborating on THE HARDY BOYS. He is a good friend and a great artist.

I have to thank him for introducing me to Papercutz and THE HARDY BOYS. The MEGAMAN series took off, and I ended up teaching Manga-style drawing to young artists at a place called Impacto Studios in Brazil.

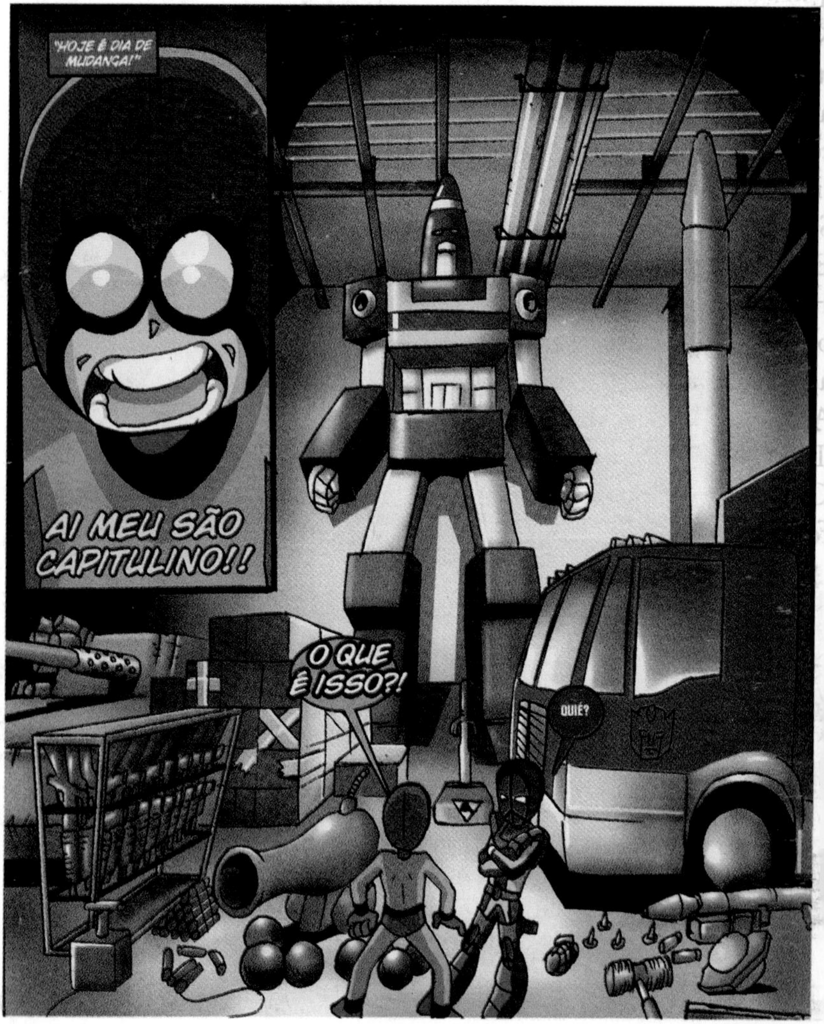
"HOJE É DIA DE MUDANÇA!"
AI MEU SÃO CAPITULINO!!
O QUE É ISSO?!
QUIÉ?